Sycamore Creek

Black Mountain

Pitchfork Ranch

Verde Valley

Jerome

Sycamore

Cottonwood

Oak Creek

Black Hills

Verde River

Oak Creek

Camp Verde

This is a fictional look at life in the old west. All characters, places or events portrayed in this book spring from the author's imagination and should never be considered as anything but fiction. Any disagreement with this proclamation will be taken under advisement.

Publication Date: August 2014
Print ISBN 978-1-938586-72-9
eBook ISBN 978-1-938586-73-6
All Rights Reserved
Copyright © 2014 by Charles Lee Lesher
http://www.charleslesher.com/

Printed in the United States of America
Writers Cramp Publishing
http://www.writerscramp.us/
Editor@writerscramp.us

Bad Day on the Verde

Double Trouble

Just as Ben and Jossy made the last turn, a lone rider came from town trailing a mule behind him. The brim of his hat was pulled low and the collar of his duster turned up hiding most everything. Only his face was partially exposed and that was in shadow.

The rider passed them on Jossy's side of the buckboard only a few feet from her. She glanced up just as a bolt of lightning sent stark shadows dancing across the most hideous face she had ever seen. She gasped loud enough for the man to hear. His eyes held hers for an instant, an image right out of a nightmare. It was an intense moment, something Jossy would never forget.

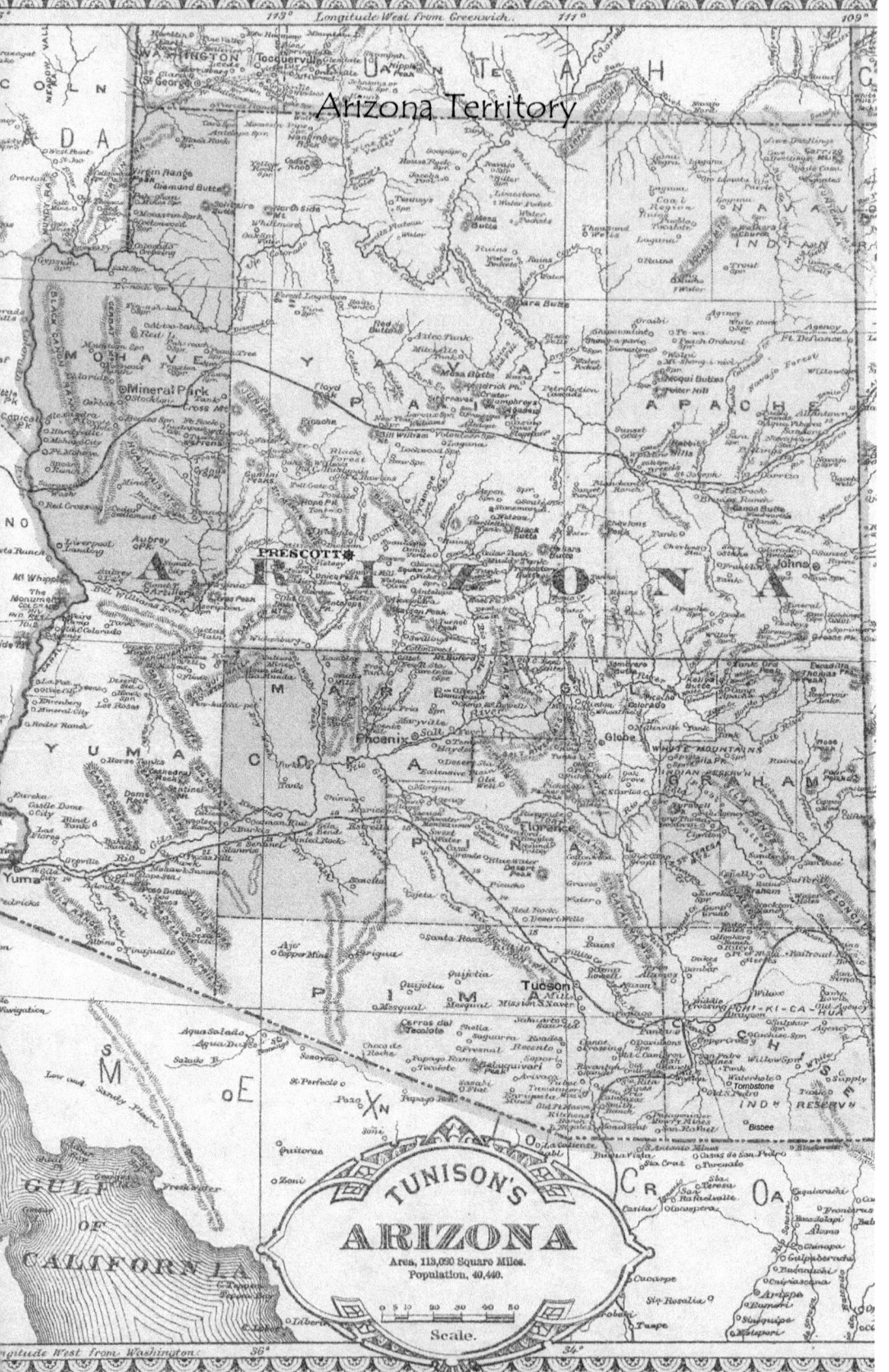

Dedication

To Peggy, the woman who brings love, happiness, and a touch of sanity into my life.

I love westerns and have been reading and enjoying them since I first learned to read for pleasure. During my stint in the army, there were times when I read a Louis L'Amour western a day. Eventually I ran out of books but the stories, or more importantly, his characters, stayed with me.

In the years since, I have started my own western novel many times and written a few short stories but it wasn't until I met Ben Miller that I finally found my inner voice and let it flow. I owe Ben a sincere and heartfelt thanks for getting me off the dime and writing my first full length western. In honor of his contribution to this book, I named one of the heroes in the book after him. It doesn't hurt that it's a perfect fit.

Bad Day is a story of violence and brutality, of sudden frontier justice, but also of courage and enduring love. The story takes place in the Arizona Territory at a time when the only law enforcement outside the capital city of Prescott was a few men wearing a star. When one of them goes bad, all hell breaks loose.

Chuck Lesher

The Players

The Lawmen

- ♣ U.S. Marshal Pete Meade
- ♣ Deputy U.S. Marshal Frank Kingsley
- ♣ Deputy U.S. Marshal Levi Watt
- ♣ Sheriff Garfias

The Outlaws

- ♣ Red Jack Almer
- ♣ Maggie Almer
- ♣ Tom Almer
- ♣ Billy Almer
- ♣ Yancy
- ♣ Al Coulter

Collateral Damage

- ♣ Ben Banyon - big square shouldered farmer and former member of the Union's Iron Brigade
- ♣ Jossy Banyon - Ben's beautiful young wife
- ♣ Emmett Perkins - Owner of Pitchfork Ranch and ex-army surgeon. Was captured at Gettysburg and sent to Elmira Prison. Fought for the South
- ♣ Hollister - Old cowboy and Pitchfork Ranch hand.
- ♣ Quinn - Sycamore's liveryman. Was sergeant in the 16th Illinois Volunteer Cavalry - Fought for the Union
- ♣ Otis - Owner and barkeep of the Tumbleweed Saloon. Lost his foot at Bull Run fighting for the South
- ♣ Angus Campbell - Farmer: A shy deliberate Scotsman with a heavy accent and a big heart. Has blond hair, is very tall and lean
- ♣ Mary Campbell - Wife of Angus.
- ♣ Warren Neally - Young gunhand from Abilene, Texas
- ♣ Doc Morris - Sycamore's doctor.
- ♣ Verónica Rodriquez de la Peña de Ybarra - owner of the Casa Espíritus, a cantina on the Mexican side of town.

Bad Day on the Verde

About Chuck

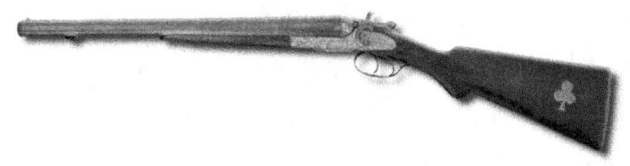

Lloyd Strong

L ife in the Arizona Territory can be unforgiving. No rain for months on end, just the relentless sun beating down on you day after day. A few hours past daybreak and the heat was already oppressive. A stray gust of hot wind whipped itself into a dust devil that danced along the street mocking the dried-out buildings. Florence may have had paint applied to it at some point in time, but if so, that time was long gone. Only a few fading signs showed any color at all.

From down the street came a group of heavily armed men. Two of them carried the strongbox between them. Trailing behind where he could keep an eye on things came the Florence sheriff. Walking alongside him was a man wearing a suit who didn't look at all happy. They all stopped next to the stage.

"Sheriff, can you guarantee this shipment will get through?" The man in the suit asked.

"John, you stick with banking and let me do my job. Lloyd here is a good man and Rand has never lost a shipment." The sheriff turned to the stage driver. "Is everything ready?"

Rand nodded and climbed inside the coach. He pulled up the forward seat cushion and unlatched the seat itself, removing it. "Hand the box up."

The two men placed the strongbox on the floor with a thump setting the coach swaying. Rand grunted when he picked it up and manhandled it into the compartment under the seat. Putting the seat and cushion back, Rand climbed down.

"All set sheriff." Rand said.

"Good. Don't forget to send a telegraph when you reach Albuquerque. Otherwise, John will have a fit."

"Just make sure it arrives. A lot depends on it, including your job." John said to Rand.

Rand frowned and would have said something, but before he could, the sheriff spoke up. "John, you need to back down."

Rand shook his head and said to his shotgun rider, Lloyd Strong. "Load the passengers and let's get out of here."

It was thirty-five miles to Jackrabbit Station where fresh horses would be waiting. The climb from Florence to Jackrabbit was brutal on a team so Rand checked and rechecked all six horses and their rigging. He found them well watered and chomping at their bits ready to go. Rand also gave the Concord stagecoach a cursory look finding nothing amiss. These coaches are so solid and well engineered that they seldom broke down, instead they just wore out.

Rand walked around the stage to where Lloyd was helping the passengers board. They only had four on this run. An older woman travelling with a teenage girl had been on the stage since Prescott. Joining them here in Florence was a rancher heading to Kansas, and a heavyset woman getting off in Globe. The girl was why Lloyd was so willing and eager to help load passengers this morning. She was quite the looker with long black hair and compelling dark eyes.

Lloyd handed the older lady up first. "Ma'am."

"Thank you, kind sir." She was old and wise enough to know what was going on. She kept her eye on things, but didn't stop it. Pleasant distractions should never be squandered.

Lloyd looked down at the girl and offered his hand. She smiled and laid hers shyly in his. The young man towered over her and practically picked her up while helping her climb into the coach inciting a surprised, but gleeful squeal.

"Ma'am." Lloyd said. His breath was warm on her cheek.

The girl was obviously impressed and that alone made Lloyd's chest puff out. That she was as interested in him as he was in her was all aces.

"Much obliged." She said smiling down at the young man from a seat inside the coach, her eyes shinning in the morning light.

Lloyd smiled back. "My pleasure, ma'am." He touched the brim of his hat.

"Move it, cowboy." The heavyset woman said, spurring Lloyd to get out of the way.

"Pardon, ma'am." Lloyd said. When he reached out to help her board, she slapped his hand.

Without another word, the woman climbed into the coach and settled opposite the girl. The rancher was last and watched everything with a detached interest. He climbed aboard and sat beside the heavyset woman.

Lloyd shut the stage door firmly, making sure it was latched, smiled at the girl one more time, and climbed up to take his place beside Rand. Something about the fat woman passenger bothered him, but he was so caught up with the girl that he didn't pursue it.

"Ain't she something, Rand? That girl is going to make someone a terrific wife." Lloyd said.

"Sure Lloyd, she sure is." Rand said. He was married almost twenty years now, but still marveled at young love. "HYAAAA." He slapped the reins across his team. Slowly at first, but picking up speed, the stage moved down the street and left Florence behind.

Inside the stage, the rancher had the same nagging bother that Lloyd had with the heavyset woman. He turned to her. "This your first time in a stage?"

The woman looked at him without speaking.

Unfazed, the rancher continued. "This is a Concord. It's roomy don't you think?" When she still didn't respond, he continued. "There's something in its roll that's like a mother rocking her baby."

She still refused to speak.

"Poetry in motion, if you ask me." The older lady accompanying the girl said.

The man nodded. "Yes ma'am. Mitch Johnson. I run a spread west of Tucson."

"Faye Owens and this is Lucy."

"Pleased to make your acquaintance." He turned to the heavyset woman. "What's your name, ma'am?"

She glanced at him then turned to look out the window, refusing to speak.

Mitch shrugged.

"Tell me more about this ranch of yours." Faye said.

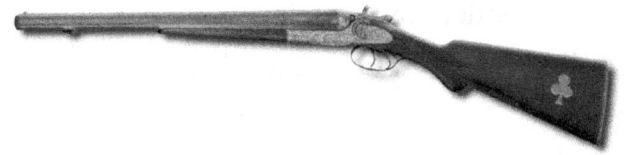

Thirty miles outside of Florence, Jackrabbit Hill presented a challenge for any team of horses. Rand let his team slow to a walk long before reaching the top. It was the main reason the relay station was at the crest of the hill. The horses were spent by the time they reached it.

Rand coaxed his team the final half mile and let them come to a stop in the station's changing yard. The horses knew they were finished for the day, they had been here before, but instead of Carlos and his cousin waiting for them with a fresh team, the yard was quiet.

Mitch opened the coach door and stepped down even before the stage came to a complete stop. He stretched then turned to help Faye.

Rand was uneasy. "Lloyd, jump down and see where that crazy Mexican is. He's probably taking a siesta."

Lloyd kept his rifle with him and climbed down just in time to help the young woman descend. He tipped his hat to Faye "Ma'am." He glanced up at the other woman who stayed in the coach then went about his business. Circling around behind the stagecoach, he was met with the blast from both barrels of a big shotgun. The twin masses of hot lead hit him just below his rib cage, cutting him in half and opening him up like a gutted steer. His spine shown white in the sea of red and his blood splattered all the way to the passengers gathered next to the stage.

The girl screamed, but before anybody could do anything,

they were surrounded by bandits, with hats pulled low over bandanas pulled high over their mouth and nose. Only their eyes were visible.

Rand was a good man, but he was out gunned and in a very vulnerable position on top of the coach. He threw his hands up. "Don't shoot. I'm unarmed. Don't shoot."

"Throw down the gold box." One of the bandits ordered.

Rand shook his head. "No box and no gold. We're carrying passengers and the mail." He climbed down.

"You're a damn liar." The heavyset woman said in a remarkably masculine voice as she exited the coach. "The gold is under the forward seat inside the stage. I saw you put it there." It was more than she had said the entire trip up to that point.

Mitch looked at her oddly. "I'll be damned. You're a man." He reached over and yanked the bonnet from her head. Sure enough, this woman was a man, a man with flaming red hair. The rancher saw the gun a moment too late. From only a few feet away, it was impossible to miss. Mitch never heard the shot that ripped through his heart.

As the rancher slumped to the ground, Faye gasped and rushed to him. The girl followed, but her tears were for Lloyd. Shock at seeing him so brutally killed was setting in. She wiped specks of blood from her face, and couldn't take her eyes from his body.

The red haired man scowled and motioned for the skinny bandit to go get the gold from inside the stage. Then he grabbed the girl by her arm. "You're coming with me."

"Now just hold on there, why take the girl?" Rand stepped forward instinctively to protect the young woman.

One of the other bandits pistol whipped Rand across the back of his head. He landed beside the dead rancher unconscious and bleeding.

"Bullies and murderers." Faye gasped. There was nothing more to do for Mitch. She left him and did what she could to stem the flow of blood from Rand's wound, ripping her petticoat for a bandage that she wrapped around his head. "This man's skull is cracked. He'll die without a doctor." Faye looked up at the man who had done it. Something's wrong with his eye.

To Faye's utter horror, the bandit raised his gun and fired a bullet into Rand. "Problem solved." The voice from behind the red bandana was deep and devoid of any human compassion.

Shear terror filled Faye. Three good men lay dead. What chance did she have?

Behind her, the skinny bandit climbed out of the stage, leaving the strong box on the floor where he could get to it. Once his feet were firmly on the ground, he pulled the box out of the coach, letting it drop with a thud. Drawing his pistol, he shot the lock open. Flipping the lid, he rummaged around inside then said to the man wearing a dress. "We'll need both saddlebags. I'd say about $3,000 in gold, Jack."

"No names." Jack hissed, but one look at Faye convinced him that she had heard. He motioned to the bandit.

Without hesitation, before she could move, the bandit raised his pistol and shot Faye in the head. "Problem solved."

Red Jack laughed. "You are one cold hombre."

The young woman screamed and couldn't stop. Red Jack slapped her hard sending her sprawling on the ground. She had never been treated so, never felt the back of a man's hand, never seen another person killed, never lost someone so close to her. She sobbed and stared at Faye then at the still warm body of the young shotgun rider a few feet away. Lloyd had been such a nice man. The driver was dead, the rancher was dead and her Faye, her precious Faye. What will she do without Faye? She had never felt this alone. She sobbed uncontrollably. The skinny bandit yanked her to her feet and the murdering bastard who had just killed Faye slammed her hard in the stomach. She fell to her knees gasping for air. It was all she could do just to breathe. She shut up but her tears never stopped.

The red haired bandit wearing a dress jerked Lucy to her feet and hissed in her ear. "I know who you are. Worth more than all the gold this lousy stage was carrying."

"How's that, Jack?" The slim bandit asked.

"This here's the governor's daughter." Jack chuckled. "How much you think that bastard will pay to get her back?"

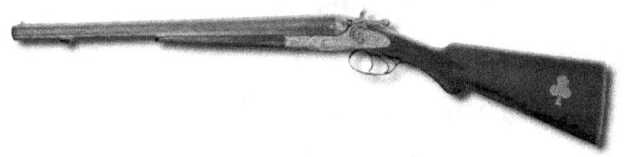

Levi Watt

Three Weeks Later

The two men stepped off their mounts in front of the Palace Livery and led them inside. Pete's dun gelding smelled the oats and followed his nose.

Levi chuckled. "Food is all that horse thinks about."

Pete nodded. "That he does." He let his horse lead him to the storage bin, opened it and scooped a generous amount into the nearest trough. Levi brought his horse over to join the dun.

"Can I help you fellers?" The voice asking belonged to a tall man with a long hound-dog face. He was wearing worn blue calvary trousers a size too large. The faded yellow stripe down each pant leg matched the faded yellow suspenders holding them up. He had been tending stock in the corrals behind the livery and held a shovel in one hand and a bridle in the other.

Pete turned to him. "Morning. I'm U.S. Marshal Pete Meade and this is Deputy Marshal Levi Watt. We would like to stable our horses tonight. A good rub down to go along with the oats."

"That'll be two dollars." The man said. His voice echoed through his huge nose and emerged in a strange nasal whine.

"That's fine." Pete grinned.

"Per horse. Two dollars per horse." The man said.

Levi laughed, and when the liveryman frowned at him, only made Levi laugh harder.

Pete smiled broadly and shook his head. "Don't mind Levi. Two dollars a night is fine. Make sure I get a written receipt "

"Yes sir, Mr. Marshal, sir."

Levi laughed even harder.

"You can call me Pete or just Marshal." But the man was already gone, leading another horse to a stall further inside the big barn muttering something under his breath.

Pete walked out of the livery with Levi beside him and pointed down Bisbee's Main Street. "Get us a room at the hotel, Levi. I will check out the Grand Saloon then meet you at Costello's café. They serve the finest beef steak this side the Mississippi. My treat."

"Sounds fine." Levi said.

"Good lad." Pete said. "I won't be long." He walked across the dusty street heading for the open front door of the saloon. Clumping up the worn wooden steps, he crossed the porch and entered the establishment. He stopped just inside to let his eyes adjust to the dimness.

It also let those inside get a good look at the gleaming silver star on his chest. A hush swept over those nearest him.

Pete grinned and showed his hands. He wasn't there to arrest anybody. At least ten men were standing at the bar and most of the tables had people, but the real action was in the back where a sizable crowd had gathered. Pete swept the room with his gaze cataloging and pigeonholing every man in sight. Only then did he make his way towards the game.

Kingsley sat with his back to the wall only a few feet from the rear door. There were four young drovers at the table with him, cards, coins and whisky arranged in front of them. Others had gathered around the table watching the game play out. Pete found a spot where he felt comfortable and settled in.

"I cover your two hundred and raise a hundred twenty."

The first player was dismayed and let it show, slapping his hand down on the table. That was more than he had left, much more. "Fold." The next did the same and the next. It left two men battling for the pot which Pete estimated to hold at least a thousand dollars. That's three years pay for a drover.

The last cowboy in the game sat there taking his time, gazing from under a broad brimmed hat at Kingsley then at his cards and back to Kingsley.

Kingsley leaned back letting the lamp light fall across his face. "Take a real good look. You're payin' for it." A thick band of scar tissue started at his scalp where his left ear should have been and curved down under his eye to his nose. Below the scar, his check slumped downward dragging the corner of his eye with it. Looking at just the side that wasn't damaged, Kingsley was an older man with graying hair and salt and pepper beard. The side with the scar was uniquely Kingsley and scared the shit out of most people, these drovers included.

Making up his mind, the cowboy leaned forward and pushed his entire pile of coins into the pot and did the same with his three friends. To their credit, they remained quiet as he bet everything. It was all they had left of their trail pay, but they trusted their friend. "Call." The young man laid his cards out face up. "Full house, tens over deuces. Let's see what you got Kingsley."

"Pot's short. The bet was a hundred and twenty dollars. All you together only had eighty." Kingsley said. The air sucked out of the room.

"You're trying to buy the pot." The young drover said.

"Table stakes, Willie. You're forty dollars short, so unless you can come up with it, you fold and the pot's mine." Kingsley said.

Willie scowled and said loudly to the room. "I'll split the pot with the first man to give me forty dollars."

Pete already had two twenty-dollar gold pieces in his hand. He tossed them on the table in front of Willie with a clatter.

Willie glanced first at Pete, then at the badge. "Thanks Marshal."

Without even looking up, Kingsley said. "You need to mind your own business, Meade."

Pete grinned. "Never been good at that."

"I called and the pot's right. Show me your hand." Willie said.

Kingsley looked up at Pete then at Willie. His poker façade collapsed into a scowl. He turned his cards over, three aces, a king and a three.

The four cowboys went nuts, whooping and hollering and jumping up and down. "Drinks all 'round." Willie called to the barkeep. The money disappeared from the table and the saloon patrons followed the jubilant cowboys to the bar knowing that the party had just begun. This left Pete and Kingsley alone at the back of the saloon. Pete took a seat across from Kingsley.

Kingsley was still scowling. "Why you here Meade?"

"To bring you this." Pete tossed the deputy marshal's badge on the table in front of Kingsley. The scowl faded away as Kingsley picked it up. The man rubbed his thumb over the spatters of dried blood still on the badge. The look of remembrance that came over Kingsley's face sent shivers through Pete. This just felt wrong, but he had no choice. The decision to return this man his badge was the governors, not his. His job was to find Kingsley, give him the badge and relay his assignment.

"The governor send you?" Kingsley asked.

Pete nodded.

"What's the catch?"

"He wants you to take care of a problem, an old friend of yours. Talking about Red Jack Almer and his brothers."

"They ain't no friends of mine." Kingsley said.

"Glad to hear it. Three weeks ago they robbed the Florence stage killing the driver, his shotgun and two passengers. The governor's daughter was taken. Red Jack demanded $10,000 and when the governor wouldn't pay, thought it was a good idea to dump her body near the new courthouse right there in Prescott. Now the governor wants them all dead."

"Can't say as I blame him. How you know it was Red Jack?"

"Several witnesses seen him in Prescott that morning and one says she fed Red Jack, Tom, Billy, Molly and the girl dinner a day or so before the body was found."

"Was she alive?" Kingsley asked.

Pete nodded. "Marta said the girl had an appetite enough for two men. She thinks they hadn't been feeding her right for the weeks since they took her."

"Marta? The old lady that cooks in the Cattleman's Hotel?" Kingsley asked.

"The same."

"Let me get this straight. Red Jack brought the girl to the hotel?" Kingsley asked.

"Seems so. Red Jack Almer will never be accused of being a genius." Pete said.

"You got that right, Meade. Red Jack's a dumb ass, through and through. It'll be pure pleasure putting a bullet in the man."

Pete stared at Kingsley. There was a deep evil here that set the warning bells in Marshal Meade to ringing. The Pete in him wanted to believe there was good in Kingsley, but if there was, it was hiding in some dark corner scared shitless. The balance in this man between good and bad was tilted noticeably towards bad. Pete almost walked away, but if he did, the governor would ask for and get a new district marshal, and he liked his job. "The governor mentioned you specifically so you get another chance. Don't blow it."

Kingsley looked over at Pete. "Why not assign Earp or Haggard to go after Red Jack?"

"They have their own assignments and like I said, the governor asked for you. Notifications to all the other Arizona lawmen has been sent out that this is your assignment. They will stay out of your way."

Kingsley nodded. "Thought so. You don't want to get your hands dirty and there's nobody else. You ain't got no more deputies to send."

"Wrong. You'll take Deputy Levi Watt with you."

Kingsley held up his hand. "Whoa, that green kid? Now wait a minute, I don't need a partner to bring down the Almers, especially someone fresh off the train. He would only slow me down and probably get himself killed."

"He's a fully qualified deputy marshal and you're taking him. That's final. And he better come back in one piece." Pete said. "You can always give me the badge back."

Kingsley scowled. "That's not going to happen."

"Right now Deputy Watt is having a steak with me at Costello's café. When he's finished he'll join you at the livery. You have that long to pull your gear together. You leave within the hour."

Kingsley scowled again. He didn't like taking anyone with him on an assignment, let alone some shavetail. He hated it almost as much as he hated taking orders from Pete Meade.

Pete stood up from the table and waited patiently until Kingsley finally gave him an almost imperceptible nod of acquiescence.

"Here's the arrest warrant." Pete laid the folded paper on the table.

Kingsley picked it up and snorted derisively. "Arrest warrant. You mean death warrant don't you Meade? It says right here, dead or alive. What do you think I'm going to do? Politely ask Red Jack to come with me so the governor can hang him?"

"Just do your job." Pete said.

"Oh, I will. You can count on it."

Like heat radiating from a bonfire, Pete felt the hostility emanating from Kingsley as he turned and walked away. But before he reached the front door, the young drover intercepted him.

"Much obliged Marshal. Here's your half." The young man held out a rawhide bag to Pete.

Pete grinned and accepted the bag of coins, opened its drawstring, removed his two gold pieces and extended the bag back to the young man.

"That's yours Marshal. Everybody here heard me say I would split it. You trying to make me look bad?"

Pete shook his head. "Not at all, but I can't accept it. By law this would be considered a bribe and I would be obligated to arrest you. Is that what you want?" Pete asked.

The young drover stared at him for a moment. "You're serious?"

Pete nodded solemnly. "I never joke about the law. Now take this and try and hold on to some of it. Put it in a bank or buy some cows of your own. Don't blow it on whisky and women."

The man accepted the bag and extended his hand. "Funny you should mention that. I'm planning to homestead and start a spread."

"Oh? Where?"

"Bighorn Basin, Wyoming. Heard it had land. Good land. I aim to see for myself."

"Sounds like you mean it. What's your name?"

"Marchant, Willie Marchant."

"Willie, good luck to you and next time, know who you are playing poker with. I may not be around." Pete turned and left the saloon. The young drover stood staring after him.

Pete clumped down the wooden walkway thinking about how that could have turned out if he hadn't been there. Not well, he imagined. Levi was waiting for him on the boardwalk just outside the cafe.

"Kingsley was there. He'll met you at the livery after we

eat." Pete said.

"Fine." Levi had been looking forward to a night between sheets. They entered the cafe and ordered their meal. Neither man tasted it much, their thoughts on what lay ahead.

Finishing his steak, Pete asked Levi. "You got any questions? Now's the time.

Levi pushed his plate back. "Just one. I seen it. Kingsley's badge. You dropped it and I seen it when I handed it back."

"Seen what?" Pete asked.

"There was blood on it. Dried blood. Whose was it?"

Pete paused and nodded. "You got a right to know, but keep in mind this is pure supposition. What I heard was the blood on the badge came from a Mexican whore that died when Kingsley played a little too rough. They couldn't prove it was him so the man walked free, but Kingsley lost his badge anyway. Now he has it back."

"Why?"

Pete shrugged. "Because the governor wants him to do what he does best."

"What's that?" Levi asked.

"Kill people." Pete said. "Make sure you ain't one of them."

"What?" Levi was taken aback.

Pete shook his head. "I ain't doing you no favors sending you with him. Just you watch your back around Kingsley. And pay attention. I will expect a full and complete report when the mission is over. Now, let's get a move on."

Kingsley's horse was ready to go and tied in front of the livery when Pete and Levi walked up. The liveryman said that Kingsley had gone for some additional supplies. Pete waited while Levi saddled his mount and led it out of the livery.

When Kingsley returned, he was carrying a bottle of cheap whisky and three boxes of 10 gauge shotgun shells, all of which he stashed in his saddlebags. Levi came over and stuck out his hand for a shake. "Levi Watt, sir."

Kingsley looked down at the hand as if it were covered in shit, brought his gaze back to the young man's face and growled in his thick gravelly voice. "Frank Kingsley."

"Oh, I know who you are. It's a pleasure to ride with you." Levi let his hand drop and backed away.

"You may change your mind on that." Kingsley said.

Kingsley's voice took some getting use to. "Ah... yes, sir." He turned to Pete. "Marshal Meade, it's been a pleasure to ride with you. See you back in Prescott." The young man gave Pete a little salute.

Pete smiled and returned the salute. "Take care Levi. Remember what I said, Kingsley. He comes back in one piece."

Kingsley and Levi stepped to their saddles and turned north spurring the horses to a long trot that ate up the miles.

They dry camped for the night about twenty miles south of Tombstone. After taking care of the horses, they sat beside a small fire eating beans and hardtack.

Levi sipped his tin of Arbuckle coffee, winced and said. "Damn, I'm glad my mother's not here to drink this. My coffee's either strong enough to stand a spoon up in it or hot water."

Frank reached into his saddlebag and tossed Levi the bottle of whiskey. "Pour a little a this in there and you'll not care."

Levi caught the bottle, but stared at Kingsley a moment too long. "What you looking at, boy?" Kingsley asked. "You looking at my face?"

Levi swallowed hard and the bottle shook as he added whisky to his coffee. "No sir."

Kingsley huffed. "If you're not, then you would be the first. What did Meade tell you?" The whole left side of his face looked like it had melted.

"That you got the scar in a fight south of the border. Must have hurt some." Levi said.

"Some, but I like pain, boy. You still got a lot to learn about pain." Kingsley replied. He then reached into his inside jacket pocket and pulled out a deck of well worn cards. "You know how to play poker?"

Levi had played some with his kin and knew the rules, but that was about all. "Sure."

Kingsley dealt the first hand giving Levi a four, a seven, an ace and two eights. "How many?" He asked.

"Ah, two cards." Levi's eyes were wide with excitement as he pulled the two cards and extended them out to Kingsley.

Kingsley ignored him and looked at his own hand. He glanced then pulled one from the five and tossed it on the ground between them face down. "Dealer takes one." He put his hand down and picked up the deck. Kingsley gave Levi two cards, dropped a fresh card on top his other four, laid down the pack and picked up his hand. "What ya got?"

"Two aces and three eights." Levi laid his hand down, face up.

"Aces and eights. Well, you sure got me beat." Kingsley threw in his hand. "A full house."

"Huh?" Levi said.

"That's what it's called, a full house. You must be plum lucky. Tell you what, anti up and you can deal the next hand." Kingsley dropped a penny on the ground between them.

Levi thought about it for a moment. "It's only a penny, right?"

"Right." Kingsley agreed and they played poker. By the end of the night, Levi had won a dollar. Kingsley made sure of it.

The next morning, they were on the trail before daybreak. Kingsley set a fast pace that discouraged talking. It was well before noon when they rode into Tombstone. At the edge of town Levi pulled up beside Kingsley and asked. "Pete also mentioned you rode with Red Jack Almer a time or two."

Kingsley shrugged. "Might have, but that don't mean nothing now." He reached down and slid his shotgun from its scabbard, laying it across his lap and against the saddle horn.

It was the biggest gun Levi had ever seen. The twin muzzles looked like he could roost his ma's chickens inside. "What kind of gun is that?"

Kingsley brought the double-barreled shotgun up and rested its butt against his hip letting Levi see it in its entirety. "This is the king of shotguns, boy. Baker 10 gauge. Baker himself made this one for me personally. See all the fancy work he cut into the iron here and the stock here?"

Levi leaned over to see better. There was a symbol inlaid into the stock, a club like what's used in cards. "Beautiful work."

"This gun will cut a man in half." Kingsley said.

Levi pulled back.

"Time to earn your pay, boy. Take off that badge and stick it in your pocket." Kingsley said.

"Uh? Why?"

Kingsley twisted in his saddle to confront Levi. "You're not here to ask questions, boy. Do what I tell you to and you might see tomorrow. No more questions." Kingsley snapped.

Levi was young and nervous, and this was his first major assignment. He literally couldn't stop himself. "Where do we start looking?"

Kingsley swung the shotgun towards Levi who kneed his horse sideways and the edge of the street. Anywhere away from this wild man.

"Fine, I got it, no more questions." This guy was crazy.

They found space among the horses tied up in front of the saloon and headed straight to the bar. The place was filled with miners and those who preyed on them, but Kingsley had no real problems plowing a path. The men moved aside as soon as they had a look at Kingsley.

The bartender spotted him as he sidled up to the bar. "Marshal Kingsley, ain't seen you in a month a Sundays."

"Ain't been around. Whiskey, bottle and glass." The barkeep sat the whiskey and two glasses in front of them. Kingsley reached in his pocket for some coin and slapped it down on the bar. "Seen Red Jack and the boys lately?"

The barkeep poured two drinks. "Not in better than three weeks. Someone, I ain't saying who, hit the stage east of Florence and I ain't seen Red Jack since." He leaned forward and lowered his voice. "I heard he might be in Prescott but you didn't hear it from me."

"He take Maggie with him?"

"Hell if I know, but I doubt he'd leave her behind."

"Yeah, kind of how I had it figured." Kingsley threw down

the drink in a single gulp. "Down the hatch boy. We ain't got all day."

Levi picked up his drink and swallowed half of it, choked and started coughing.

The barkeep had a good laugh. Kingsley poured himself another and downed it just like the first, in a single gulp. "You keep this little conversation to yourself, you hear me?" He picked you the bottle of whiskey and his shotgun.

"Sure, anything you say, Marshal." The barkeep watched Kingsley leave his saloon and wondered about the kid. He had never seen Kingsley with a partner before. It didn't feel right somehow.

Back at their horses, Kingsley put the fresh bottle of whisky in his saddlebag and mounted. Heading north, the marshal set a blistering pace. It was all Levi could do to keep up and he knew better than to ask any questions.

It was late afternoon the next day when the two men rode into the outskirts of Tucson. "Boy, take the horses over to the livery. Have them grained and rubbed down." He got his shotgun and stepped to the sidewalk, looking the street over.

"Fine. Where will you be?"

Instead of snapping at Levi for asking yet another question, he answered him. "Loweman's Saloon. If Red Jack came through here, that's where he would have stopped."

Half an hour later, Levi found Kingsley sitting at a table with one of the saloon girls, a pretty, dark-haired Mexican younger than Levi. "Any sign of..."

"Stop right there." Kingsley said. "You will keep your mouth shut. Am I clear on this?"

Levi was taken aback. "I was just going to ask if there was any signs of a meal around here. I'm starved. I need something to eat that isn't hardtack or beans." Levi said.

"You go ahead. Oh, and get us separate rooms upstairs. Her I like, you, not so much." Kingsley said and put his arm around the girl.

Levi arranged the rooms and ordered a steak, but when he returned to the table, Kingsley and the girl didn't pay him no mind. His steak arrived a few minutes later, but they didn't speak or look at him once while he ate. By the time he finished, the girl was sitting in Kingsley's lap, and his hands were all over her.

"I'm beat. I'm going to turn in." Levi said.

Only when he stood up did Kingsley acknowledge his presence. "Boy, what's my room number? My key?" He snapped his fingers.

"Nine. Here's the key. I'm in three." Levi handed Kingsley his key and couldn't get away fast enough to suit him. He headed upstairs. He was bone tired, but couldn't stop thinking about the marshal. Kingsley was not what he had expected after talking to Marshal Meade.

Back in the saloon. "I want you to spend the rest of the night with me." Kingsley told the girl.

"Si senor, if you have the deniro."

Kingsley stiffened. "Don't you worry about the money. You'll be well paid."

Twenty minutes later in room nine, Kingsley watched the girl strip. She hung her dress on a hook back of the door and climbed onto the bed, waiting. Kingsley made sure the door was locked and leaned his Baker against the wall close to hand. Next came the gun belt. He laid it down so as to easily get to the gun if need be. The knife in his boot stayed there when his boots came off. Only then did he remove his own clothes leaving them in a pile on the floor.

"That is a very big gun, senor." The girl said.

Kingsley joined her in bed.

After kissing and wrestling around for a few minutes, the girl said. "Let me help." She started to go down on him.

Instead of letting her, it set Kingsley off. He violently pinned her to the bed using his weight advantage and superior strength. Straddling her he said. "You want to help? I know just how you can help." He punched her in the face starting her nose to bleed. A second blow broke a tooth and gashed his left hand in the process. Kingsley had learned long ago to hit whores with his non-shooting fist. While she was dazed, he forced her legs apart, and penetrated her.

The girl started to scream, but Kingsley's big hands closed around her neck shutting her up. She struggled weakly beneath him, her eyes bugging out of her face.

With a skill born of experience, Kingsley brought her right to the edge of darkness, then let her breathe. The girl gasped, her mind chaotic with death so close at hand. He repeated this again and again, pounding his manhood into her slack body working towards his climax. Finally, his eyes rolled back in his head and he emitted a low rhythmic growl that stretched out into a high frequency moan in tune with his final wild thrusts. His lust appeased, he lay on top of her for a moment then raised himself off the girl and reached for his clothes.

By the time he was dressed, the saloon girl had regained

consciousness, but all she could do was lay there gazing blankly up at Kingsley. She was confused and didn't understand what had just happened to her. Her throat was the worst. She could barely swallow. Her body ached and her face hurt.

"Lo que no?" She croaked.

He leaned down and the beaten girl cringed away in fear. "Yo soy tu peor diablo. Mind what you say or I'll be back to finish you." He laid a twenty dollar gold piece on the bed. The frightened girl snatched it up before Kingsley had time to leave the room.

Shotgun in hand, Kingsley walked down the hallway and into Levi's room without knocking. "Let's go, boy." He kicked the bed hard.

Levi sat up, all sleepy-eyed. "Yeah, what's going on?"

"Get dressed. It's time to ride."

Levi swung his legs off the side of the bed and started dressing. "Damn, it feels like I just got to sleep."

"You slept long enough. Now quit your bellyaching."

"Bellyaching? I ain't bellyaching. I just…"

"Shut the hell up and let's go." Kingsley walked out.

It was the middle of the night, and if not for the moon, it would have been hard saddling the horses. An hour on the road and Levi had to ask. "Why the hell did we ride out and it's still hours till daybreak?"

"What did I tell you about questions?" Kingsley didn't expect an answer.

Levi studied him when the blistering pace allowed. Even in this bad light and moving fast, he was sure he could see blood splattered all over Kingsley's face and arms. And his left hand was wrapped in a bloody cloth. The man had been in a fight, that was sure.

They came upon the Santa Cruz River just before daylight, watering the horses and filling their canteens. Kingsley knelt to wash his face and hands, but not before Levi seen the blood all over them. Sure enough, he had gotten into a fight, but after the deputy cleaned up, his face had no cuts or bruises. Only his left hand showed any damage indicating that someone else had taken the beating, not Kingsley. Levi filed it away, feeling a dread settle over him. Something wasn't right here.

They followed the river northwest to Casa Grande, but well before they got there, Levi knew to keep his mouth shut. Every time he tried talking, Kingsley damn near snapped his head off. He was there to follow orders; Kingsley's orders.

Riding into Casa Grande, Kingsley said. "Boy, go to the livery and get us a pack mule. We'll need more supplies than we can carry in our saddle bags. Here's ten dollars." Kingsley gave him a ten dollar gold piece. "Let's see how you haggle. Bring the mule down to the dry goods store."

Levi did as he was told and went to buy a mule. He looked them all over and picked the one he wanted, then set out to get his price. He bought the animal for nine dollars. The liveryman had a son the same age as Levi and gave him a good deal.

Tying the mule and his horse alongside Kingsley's in front of the mercantile, Levi went inside. There was a stack of supplies on the counter and Kingsley was directing the storekeeper on what he wanted next.

Levi handed the dollar to Kingsley who accepted it without a word.

They packed the supplies and were back on the trail in an hour. From Casa Grande, they followed the stage road north to the little town of Phoenix.

Well after sundown, the heat was still oppressive. "It's nighttime. How can it be this hot?" Levi asked. "This place is hell on earth, if you ask me."

"No one asked you." Kingsley said. The marshal led them to Washington Street, the heart of Whisky Row. There seemed to be a saloon on every corner and there were a lot of corners. He stepped out of his saddle and handed his reins to Levi. "Boy, find a livery and take care of the horses. And get us a room. We'll be staying the night."

"Where will you be?"

"Capital Saloon, right there." He tipped his hat towards the largest and busiest establishment in sight. Light and music streamed from its windows and open doors.

There was a boisterous crowd inside the saloon, and someone was banging away on a piano. He pushed his way to the bar and ordered whisky. Taking the bottle, Kingsley found an empty table and sat down. He gulped a drink and looked around, cataloging and analyzing every man in the room. There was a group of miners around the piano, some farmers at the end of the bar, and a rough collection of drifters and no-accounts everywhere else. A few he knew, but they knew him too and stayed their distance. They warned their friends and word spread.

"Hey friend, that's my table." The man wasn't wearing a gun and all he could see of Kingsley was the top of his hat. "I just went outside to make water."

Kingsley looked up and the man stepped back, startled. "Fine by me, you take the table." He disappeared into the crowd, discretion the better part of valor.

A few minutes later, a slender well-built Hispanic man made his way through the saloon headed for Kingsley. The look on his face wasn't exactly hostile, but it wasn't friendly either. He wore a badge.

"Deputy Kingsley. What brings you to Phoenix?"

"Howdy Sheriff. Marshal business. Hunting the Almers." Kingsley replied. "Pull up a chair and have a drink."

Sheriff Garfias would rather drink with a rattlesnake. "The Almers passed through about three weeks ago. If you hurry, you just might catch them."

Kingsley pushed his hat back on his head. "You trying to tell me to leave town?"

"People die around you, Kingsley. I just don't want to do the paperwork." Sheriff Garfias replied.

Kingsley didn't like Mexicans, but this one had a badge and a growing reputation as a fast gun, but he didn't have time to answer as all hell broke loose behind the sheriff.

Sheriff Garfias turned and was confronted with a massive fist fight just getting under way. He started for it intending to stop the free-for-all before it did too much damage. Pushing his way into the fracas, he came face to face with a much larger man who said to him. "Look who's here. You start dancing and you'd better cut some fancy steps ahead of this lead." The bigger man made a move for his gun.

"Don't do it." Sheriff Garfias warned him.

Either the man wasn't aware of Sheriff Garfias' six-gun skills or he was too drunk to care. He started to draw. His pistol had barely cleared leather when Garfias shot him dead.

The fighting stopped at the sound of gunfire and the heavy body hitting the floor. In the sudden quiet, Kingsley said to Sheriff Garfias in his gravely bass voice. "I can honestly say Sheriff, it's been a pleasure." His self-satisfied expression sent a chill across the room. Almost wistfully, he turned and walked out, the crowd parting to let him through.

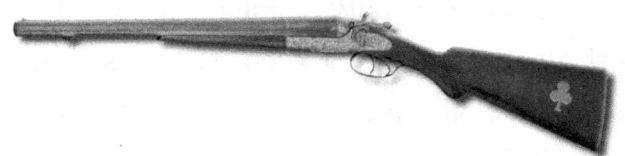

After riding many days on some of the most beautiful trails in the Arizona Territory, Kingsley and Levi arrived in Prescott. It was early afternoon. Most of the town had finished eating and was relaxing or taking siesta. The lawmen left their horses and the mule at the livery with instructions to treat the animals right, then found a café. They were hungry for a good meal. Eating on the trail was a simple affair and sitting down to a thick steak and a mess of potatoes was a welcome respite. Emerging from the cafe, the two men stood on the wooden boardwalk and gave the capital of Arizona a once over.

Time on the trail had softened Kingsley a bit, enough for him to say. "Boy, I feel like bendin' an elbow. Join me?"

"Thought you'd never ask." Levi walked beside Kingsley to the Palace Saloon wondering when he would stop calling him boy. He knew better than to ask.

Seconds after entering the bar, Kingsley knew that Red Jack wasn't here. Stepping up to the bar, Kingsley ordered a drink. He motioned to one of the saloon girls, holding up a silver dollar.

When she came over, he said. "This is yours if you can tell me a thing or two."

"I'll try, mister."

"We're looking for some folks; five men and a pretty woman, long black hair. One of the men is a breed." Kingsley said.

"Who wants to know?" The girl was suspicious.

Kingsley lays the coin on the bar. "The law." He opened his duster showing her his deputy marshal badge.

The girl glanced at the barkeep who was watching from a distance ready to grab up the shotgun he kept under the bar if need be. She shifted her gaze to the younger man who seemed to just be along for the ride. The girl shrugged. No skin off her nose if this lawman finds the Almers. "Is the woman's name Maggie?"

Kingsley nodded.

"Sure, I seen them. They was here off and on for a couple weeks or so. I think they went to Jerome." The girl said.

"You think? Can you be sure?" Kingsley asked gruffly.

She furtively looked around, then leaned close to Kingsley. "They was flush, at least that's what Maggie said."

"Did they say when they was coming back?"

The girl shook her head.

"Did they mention where they was going?" When the girl hesitated, he repeated. "Best you tell me what I want to know." He pulled a twenty dollar gold piece from his pocket and fiddled with it.

The girl's eyes lit up. "Billy mentioned a cabin northeast of Jerome, somewhere in the Verde Valley. They was going to lay low for a spell. Billy wanted me to go with them, but he's just a boy. I said no."

"Smart girl." Kingsley said. "Did they have a kid with them? A girl?"

The saloon girl frowned. "A kid? I never seen no kid with them."

"How about a young woman, say sixteen or seventeen?" Levi asked.

Kingsley glared at him and after the girl shook her head, he asked. "Were they all in here at the same time?" Kingsley held the gold piece so the girl couldn't miss it.

The saloon girl shrugged. "I have no idea."

"Think." Kingsley said.

The girl shook her head. "No, I can't recall ever seeing Tom and Billy together, now that you mention it. Why is that important?"

Kingsley put the gold piece back in his pocket and laid a second silver dollar beside the first. "You earned this."

"Hey, hold on there. That twenty is mine."

Faster than a striking rattler, Kingsley grabbed her wrist causing her to gasp. He pulled her close where his hot breath washed over her. Struggling against his immense strength, fear replaced greed as she realized the depth of coldness in this man. It was more than just his face that was scared and disfigured. It went soul deep. It was like staring in the eyes of the grim reaper himself, cold, impersonal and empty. She made up her mind in that instant, she wanted nothing to do with Kingsley, gold or no gold.

"Kingsley, she's..." Levi didn't get to finish. Kingsley cuffed him up side his head hard enough to knock him back and make his head spin. It did no real damage except to Levi's pride.

"Don't ever do that again, boy." Kingsley growled maintaining his iron grip upon the girl.

"Easy Kingsley. I'm sure Levi didn't mean a thing." Levi, Kingsley and the girl all turn to look at the man speaking.

Kingsley released the girl who immediately scooped up the two silver dollars and scurried away.

"God damn it, Meade? How the hell did you beat us here?" Kingsley asked.

Pete wasn't nearly as tall as Kingsley, slimmer in the hips and over a hundred pounds lighter. The Territorial Marshal badge gleamed on his chest. He ignored the question and turned to the young deputy. "Welcome back Levi. I trust your trip was uneventful?"

Still feeling Kingsley's blow, Levi shrugged. "We followed them here." His head felt like the inside of an Indian war drum.

"Answer me Meade, what are you doing here?" Kingsley growled.

Turning back to him, Meade replied. "Relax Frank. I'm doing what the governor ordered, just like you."

"The governor said this was my job. I don't need no help from you, and you can keep your little spy here. I don't want him coming with me. He doesn't follow orders worth a shit."

"What?" Levi couldn't believe what he was hearing.

"That's not going to happen. Levi will stay with you until this is through. When the governor learned you was in town, he sent me to fetch you."

"Well, ain't you the little messenger boy."

Pete stiffened. "He wants to see you right now so if you want to keep that badge, you need to get a move on."

"Why? What's the point?" Kingsley asked.

Pete shrugged. "He didn't tell me. You coming or not?"

Kingsley scowled. "Boy, get us rooms at St. Michaels. I'll be back shortly."

"I will follow your orders to the letter." Levi replied.

"See that you do." Kingsley said.

"Don't take it personal, Levi. He hates everybody."

Levi shrugged and watched the two men walk away. This is not how he envisioned his first assignment.

"You're pretty hard on Levi." Pete said matching stride with Kingsley. "He's a fine young man."

"Here's an idea, Meade, you take him and then you can coddle him any way you like." Kingsley said. "I know where to find the governor. You done your duty, now get lost."

Pete stopped on the boardwalk and let Kingsley go on alone. *'What a total jackass,'* Pete thought.

The courthouse was only a short walk away and Kingsley well known within its walls.

"The governor's expecting you. Go right in." The scrawny little man said from his desk outside the governors office.

Kingsley didn't acknowledge the secretary had said anything or even break stride, but opened the door and entered the room.

The governor was behind his desk looking out a window. He turned when Kingsley entered, but didn't say a thing when the lawman went straight for the decanted liquor and poured himself a stiff drink.

Kingsley held up the full glass in a mock salute. "To your continued good health." He gulped half of it down.

The governor winched. "Have you found Almer yet?"

"If I had, he'd be dead." Kingsley came over to sprawl upon the overstuffed chair near the desk.

"I've changed my mind. I want you to bring him in alive."

Kingsley's eyes narrowed. "Why?"

The governor of the Arizona Territory arose from his desk and moved to stand at the window, his back to Kingsley. "I want the people to see the law work even for me, their governor."

Kingsley clicked his tongue as if scolding an errant child. The governor turned from the window to look at him. "I thought so. You want to turn your own daughter's death into a political gold mine." Kingsley shook his grizzled head. "Governor, what you want is a nice long trial so everybody will remember your name come election time."

The governor bristled at that. "*I want justice!* Besides, territorial governors are not elected, they are appointed."

Kingsley shrugged and stood up. "Oh sure, but states have elections, don't they?" He moved to tower over the governor.

What a god-awful big man this was. The governor resisted the urge to back up and stood his ground. "Deputy Kingsley, your orders are to bring Red Jack Almer in alive. Can you do that?" Seen up close, Kingsley's disfigurement was truly hideous. The governor swallowed hard, but stayed put.

"Sure, I can do that." Kingsley said.

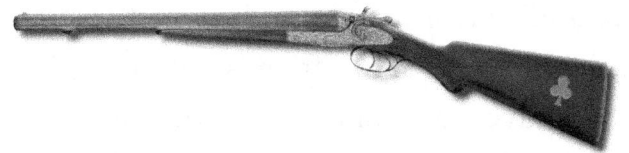

Leaving town before dawn the next morning, the two lawmen made good time crossing Prescott Valley and pitched camp that night at the foot of Mingus Mountain. Kingsley arose well before dawn and had them on the trail through the Black Hills. It took them most of the morning to climb up to Jerome.

The town's Main Street was literally cut in the side of the hill. Homes and business' were haphazardly scattered above and below the road. People, horses and mining equipment were everywhere. The bustle gave the town an air of prosperity. They tied up near a busy saloon and went in for a drink.

Finding a spot at the bar, they ordered whisky and looked around. There were maybe forty men, mostly miners, and at least that many gamblers and saloon girls looking to take their hard-earned money. The two men standing next to them at the bar smelled like sheep herders. Kingsley sniffed and took his bottle to a table near the end of the bar with two men and a girl sitting at it. Levi followed.

Kingsley didn't say a word, just set his bottle on the table and took the only open chair. Moments later the men found some excuse and left taking the girl with them. It wasn't long before Kingsley had found his own girl to sit with him, someone who found his face bearable and his money spendable. Levi again felt like a third wheel, but stuck it out.

Kingsley hit the bottle pretty hard that afternoon and was buying drinks for the girl and her friends. All the time he quietly pumped them all for information. The first saloon girl didn't know anything, but one of her friends did. Kingsley asked her. "Red Jack still have that cabin in the Verde Valley?"

"The cabin's still there, but Red Jack ain't." The woman said.

"He ain't? Where's he?"

"A shallow grave. He was killed holding up a stage."

Kingsley frowned. "How you know that?"

The woman shrugged. "Billy Almer came in here less than a week ago and told everyone about it. Billy sometimes drinks a little too much, if you know what I mean."

"Then I guess Tom and Billy are staying at the cabin?"

"I reckon."

"Where exactly is this cabin?" Kingsley asked.

"Never been there myself, but I hear it's down the hill. Stick to the stage road until you get to the water station. The cabin is due north of there about five miles."

"Five miles, you say." Kingsley bought another round and a bottle for the trail. "Never can have too much whisky." He tipped his hat to the disappointed saloon girl.

They finished their drinks and walked to their horses. As they mounted, Levi asked. "Think Red Jack is dead?"

"Only one way to find out. Let's go ask his next of kin. If he is then Red Jack's widow may be in need of some sympathy. She sure is a pretty gal. Been meaning to do her for quite some time."

That didn't sit well with Levi, but he didn't say anything. The more time he spent with Kingsley, the less he liked him.

It was all downhill from Jerome. As the crow flies, the cabin was only a couple miles from Jerome, but in this country, only a crow could take the direct route. Several hours had passed when they finally found the cabin. Tucked back in some tress, it was almost invisible until you were right on it. A dilapidated barn with a decent corral made up a little yard of sorts, but they all could use some repair.

From a ridge above the cabin, Kingsley and Levi watched Tom ride away. He was heading off to the east towards the Verde River.

"Shouldn't we go after him?" Levi asked.

"We will, boy. I want to see if the others are in the cabin." Kingsley replied. Something in his tone gave Levi a foreboding.

"I don't see any horses in the corral. Maybe they're all gone." Levi said.

They eased down the hill and tied their horses out of sight behind the ramshackle old barn.

"You stay here and keep an eye out for Tom. Wouldn't want him coming back early and surprising me." Kingsley said.

Kingsley grinned and Levi felt hell freeze over. Something was going on here that Kingsley wasn't sharing. Levi reasoned that this man was a Deputy U.S. Marshal and if you can't trust him, who can you trust? , but Levi being the curious soul that he was, just couldn't help himself. He had to ask. "What are you going to do?"

The look that came over Kingsley's face was nuclear. "Do what I tell you. Stay here and watch for Tom Almer."

"Yes sir." He didn't sound convinced.

Kingsley stepped close to Levi and got in his face. "You do what I tell you, boy. You hear me?" The warning was clear.

Levi backed down. "Yes sir." This time he meant it, more or

less.

Kingsley stared at Levi for a moment as if making up his mind on something, then turned and started for the cabin.

Levi breathed a sigh of relief and watched him leave.

Kingsley made his way around the barn and sidled up along the cabin to its door. It was unlocked so he opened it fully looking around inside. Seeing no one, he entered and walked around the table towards the bedroom, the cabin's only other room. Just as he was reaching for the knob, the door opened and Maggie emerged. She froze when she saw Kingsley and her mouth dropped open, but before she could even blink he knocked her senseless. She landed in a heap on the floor beside bed.

Kingsley searched the cabin to make sure they were alone then picked Maggie up and threw her on the bed. He began ripping her clothes off. A strange twisted sound rose from his throat as if he were a child opening a birthday present.

As the last stitch of clothing left Maggie's body, she came to. Realizing what was happening to her and by whom, she screamed at the top of her lungs.

Kingsley cut it short with another powerful left, crushing the bone in her cheek and knocking her unconscious. Blood flowed and soaked into the handmade mattress.

Levi heard the scream and came running. Gun drawn, he bolted through the open cabin door and saw Kingsley in the bedroom standing over the naked woman. He hollered. "KINGSLEY! *What the hell...*" The muzzle flash from the bedroom greeted his words.

Kingsley turned and fired, hitting Levi high in the chest. The big slug ripped into the boys body knocking Levi backwards.

He somehow managed to keep his feet under him and turned to Kingsley with a look of shocked disbelief. The deputy calmly took aim shot him again, this time low, in the stomach. Levi bent over and stumbled back out the door. He fell on the front porch of Red Jack Almer's cabin.

Kingsley came out and kneeled beside the young man gazing into his face. Levi couldn't speak, but worked his mouth like a fish out of water, his eyes pleaded with the marshal.

"You should a done what I told you. This is your own fault." Kingsley said. He leaned down close to the boys face to watch his life flicker and die.

"*Ahhhhhh!*" A sound of pure pleasure rumbled from deep in his throat at the instant of Levi's death. He closed his eyes for just a moment. "God, I love killing." Kingsley said.

He stood up and walked back into the cabin. His work for the day wasn't done.

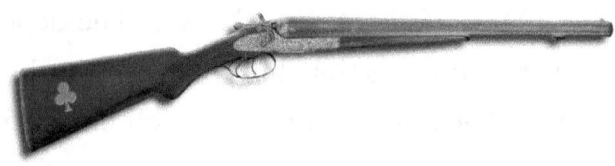

Tom Almer

Tom Almer heard the shots and turned his horse back to the cabin. Instead of racing into the yard, he jumped from the saddle well back and moved forward quiet. The first thing he saw was the body lying half on the porch and down the steps. Blood was pooling on the footpath at the bottom of the stairs.

The part of the deadman's face Tom could see wasn't familiar to him. Maggie could have shot the guy, it wouldn't have been her first kill, but he stayed cautious. He drew his gun and stepped through the open cabin door. Coming in from bright daylight, it took a few seconds for his eyes to adjust to the dim interior light. Tom compounded his mistake when he cocked his pistol. For the second time in as many minutes, a muzzle flash from the bedroom changed a life.

Kingsley heard the click and cat quick, drawing as he turned, he fired. The cabin was less then thirty feet front to back, close range for a Colt. His shot hit Tom in the right biceps ripping through muscle, narrowly missing the bone, but rendering the arm useless. Tom's gun dropped to the cabin floor. Kingsley cocked his pistol to finish the job, but before he could, Maggie hit him with everything she had, pummeling him about the head and shoulders and screaming.

Tom didn't wait to see what happened. He ducked back out the door and ran. He mounted his horse with his one good arm and lit out like he had the devil himself on his tail. He would find his brother. Jack would kill that bastard Kingsley.

Back in the cabin, Kingsley easily subdued Maggie with a pair of savage lefts then stood, looking down at her. She returned his stare defiantly, blood pouring from a smashed nose. "Jack is going to kill you, King." Her voice was slurred from the pounding she had just endured.

"I have been looking forward to this for a long time." He penetrated her roughly in one deep stroke. "You whores are all alike, ever last one. You deserve what you get." Kingsley said.

His big hands found her throat as he thrust into her. She could do nothing against his choking grip, bringing her to the point of losing consciousness, but not quite. She floated in this never-never land unable to do anything but survive.

Kingsley hammered his manhood into Maggie, all the while skillfully choking her to the brink of death. Finally, his eyes rolled back in his head and he opened his mouth wide, emitting a low rhythmic growl that turned into a high frequency moan matching his increasingly frantic thrusts. *"Ahhhhhh!"* He ejaculated his seed inside her.

His lust appeased, he lay on top of her for a few moments then raised himself off the woman, pulled up his pants and cinched his holster.

Maggie had partially recovered by the time he was ready to

leave. She lay on the bed and watched without saying a word, sure that death was coming, yet hoping he would just leave. The marshal came back to the foot of the bed to look down at the woman.

Maggie could see what was coming the instant before it arrived. "No!" She held her hands out as if they would shield her or she could push him away.

Kingsley was fast, had never been beaten in a fair fight and never fought fair. He drew and fired point blank aiming for Maggie's bellybutton. His bullet went through her outstretched hand and struck her in the abdomen tearing through her guts.

Maggie's scream turned into a moan and she clutched at her stomach, all of which meant nothing to Kingsley. He brought his face close to hers and watched the pain.

"You bastard." Maggie croaked. She died looking at Kingsley, hate warping her expression.

Kingsley locked eyes with her to the end. "*Ahhhhhh!*" He brought his face down close to hers. "Maggie, I knew you would be a sweet kill." He stood up. Never did he enjoy living as much as right after a kill, but all good things must come to an end. He left a calling card on the bed then turned away without another glance at the empty shell he left behind.

Calmly, deliberately, the lawman went through the cabin looking for anything that could help him find the others or the others find him. Just to be safe, every scrap of paper he found went into the cooking stove fire. Stopping outside on the steps, he rifled through the pockets of Levi's still warm body taking his money and papers. He removed the boy's badge from his shirt pocket and transferred it to his own. Levi's gun and holster went over his shoulder.

Kingsley went behind the barn to where they had left the horses. He removed the rifle, saddlebags and canteen from Levi's horse putting them on the mule then loosened the cinch, swinging the saddle off and dropping it to the ground. He removed the bridle and gave it a toss into some dense bushes then pointed the horse in the general direction he wanted it to go and slapped it hard on the rump. "HAYA" It galloped off. The saddle followed the bridle into the bushes.

Kingsley knew he had wounded Tom, which greatly increased his chances of running him down. He could afford to take his time. "One down, five to go." He felt on top of the world. Two kills in one day.

A couple miles away, Tom wrapped his arm in his bandana, but he knew he was in trouble. Every step his horse made sent pain radiating from his damaged arm. He didn't think he could outrun Kingsley, but he did think he could outfox him. He picked a spot that he thought would be impossible to find and left the stage road. Tom headed towards an abandoned cabin he knew about.

An hour later Kingsley found Tom's trail. He has tracked many men and looked at the obvious places where Tom's horse could have left the road until he finally came upon it. *'Stupid bastard thinks I don't know his tricks?'* Kingsley followed the tracks until dark and made camp.

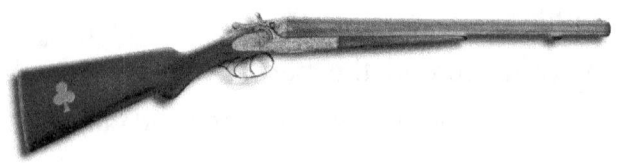

Later that night, Red Jack Almer, Billy Almer, John Coulter, and the breed, Yancy, rode in pitch blackness into the cabin's yard. It was well past sundown and dense storm clouds blocked any moonlight from getting through.

"It's as dark as the inside of a horse's ass." Billy said.

"Shut up, Billy. Something's not right." Red Jack said.

Red Jack's senses were at full alert. Not a sound from the barn and there was no lanterns lit inside the house. Maggie always left one burning low in the window when she knew he was coming in. Something was wrong, Red Jack could feel it. He pulled up outside the corral and stepped down. The others followed suit.

Billy didn't like to be told to shut up, even from his big brother. "Eat shit, Jack."

Yancy also sensed something amiss. He decided that getting away from his outlaw friends might be a good idea right about now. "I'll take care of the horses." Yancy gathered up the others reins and led the four horses away, using them as shields. He headed for the corral.

When Red Jack got to the cabin steps he nearly tripped over the dead man. A word burst unbidden from his throat. "*Shit!*" He knelt beside the body, gently turned it over and in near total darkness, stared into the face of a man he had never seen before. He stood up, calling out. "TOM, MAGGIE!"

Coulter hung back, his pistol drawn, wishing his boss would

stop yelling. If something was wrong and this was a trap, yelling would be the last thing to do.

Billy drew his gun, finally convinced that this was not a normal homecoming.

Red Jack rushed through the open cabin door and headed straight to the back room. It was just too dark to see anything, so he fumbled around lighting a lamp. He found Maggie lying on the blood-soaked bed, naked, a bullet hole in her gut. Red Jack grabbed her, clutching her to his chest. He rocked back and forth, calling her name. There, next to her pillow, the Queen of Clubs.

Red Jack picked the card up. *"Kingsley!"* Red Jack felt like his head was going to explode. Hate filled him to overflowing. Yet, he was gentle as he eased Maggie back on the bed. *"I'm going kill that son of a bitch!"*

"Who?" Billy asked from the doorway.

"Kingsley. He gut-shot Maggie." Coulter responded having entered the bedroom with Jack and watched the whole thing. He had no love for Kingsley, but that didn't mean he wanted to go look for him. Jack can always find another woman.

"Maggie's dead? " Billy came in to stare at the body.

Red Jack pulled the sheet over her and glared at him then left the room.

Yancy had entered the cabin and lit another lamp and started to look around. He found Tom's gun lying to one side and the blood on the floor. Red Jack came over to look at it. "How you read this?"

Yancy raised his lantern and walked through the tiny cabin looking at everything, but paying particular attention to the body on the front stoop. "Two men arrived, one man killed the other then shot Tom. Tom dropped his gun and ran." He pointed at the trail of blood drops through the cabin door. "Tom was wounded, but alive when he left." Yancy didn't say anything about Maggie or what happened to her. He knew when to hold his tongue.

"We're going to ride that bastard into the ground. I just hope Tom got away." Billy said.

"Don't you fret about that. Your brother is a hard man to kill." Red Jack replied.

"I'm thinking Tom will head for Camp Verde and wait for us." Billy said.

"Might at that. We'll rest the horses a few hours then hit the trail at daybreak. Shouldn't be hard to find the bastard. He's wearing a badge."

Yancy and Coulter exchanged glances. Neither wanted a showdown with the law, especially one with Kingsley. They had both had their fill of the man and would just as soon stay clear, but they would go along for now.

The next morning, right at daybreak, they laid Maggie to rest under a makeshift cross north of the cabin, beside a young man nobody knew. Red Jack was the last to step up on his horse. He looked down at the fresh graves. "He'll pay, Maggie. As God is my witness, he'll pay."

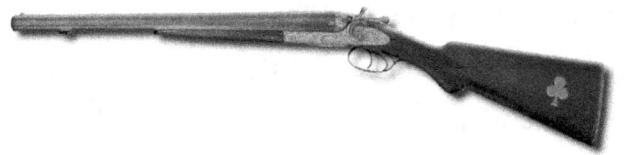

Tom kept riding well into the night, letting his horse pick its way. Lightning flashed on the horizon providing glimpses of what lay ahead. On he rode into the darkness, his arm in constant pain. Just before midnight, the rain started out light, then built to a downpour. He was wet through and through by the time a lightening flash revealed the old cabin. He tied his horse to a tree close by and stumbled inside. Someone had used the cabin recently. The old fireplace had been cleaned out and a small pile of dry wood was beside it. That same someone had cleared space for a bedroll and even left a few supplies on a shelf.

It was there that Tom found a box of sulfur matches. Building a fire, he hunkered down close. He should remove the saddle from his horse, but he didn't have the energy. Same with his clothes, it just wasn't worth the effort. They would dry on his body or stay wet. He didn't care which right now.

His wound was a through and through, but Tom was smart enough to know he needed a doctor. He used part of his shirt to bandage the bullet hole, front and back. It had stopped bleeding, but still hurt like the devil.

Tom rummaged through the remaining supplies and found a few pieces of hardtack. "God damned jawbreaker." He muttered to himself. It was full of worms, but he was too hungry to care. He wolfed it down and then added more wood to the fire.

He placed his hat on the floor and lay down close to the stove. He was dead tired. In no time, he dropped off to sleep.

Long before dawn, the cold awoke him and he added more wood to the red hot coals. The little pile of firewood was almost gone. His shirt and trousers were dry on the side facing the stove, so he turned around to let his other side dry. If anything, his arm was worse, a constant pain that never went away.

As dawn broke, Kingsley had a small fire going and coffee water on. His horse and mule were tied nearby, soaked to the bone. The rain had washed away any trail left by the outlaw. It only made his job harder, not impossible.

But just when he had come to grips with that, Kingsley spotted something near the bottom of the canyon. There, through the trees, he could barely make out a rundown cabin with Tom's bay horse tied to a nearby sapling. "Well, damn my hide." Kingsley muttered.

He broke camp and saddled his horse, tightened the pack cinch on the mule and made his way down the side of the steep canyon. It took him over an hour, but the bay hadn't moved when he was again in sight. He tied up well away from the cabin's closed door and pulled his Baker shotgun from its scabbard. He broke the gun and removed the two shells, looking at them closely. Satisfied, he reloaded then rested his thick thumb on the twin hammers ready to pull them back at the first sign of trouble. He started for the cabin keeping quiet. The closer he got, the more cautious he became.

He paused outside the door listening for several long moments before reaching out and carefully lifting the latch. When the latch released, Kingsley pushed the door wide open and leapt into the room.

Lying awake on the floor, Tom cried out and made a weak play for his Winchester. He was stopped abruptly by the butt of Kingsley's heavy shotgun. Tom slumped back, dazed and bleeding. Kingsley relieved Tom of the rifle.

"I could of killed you, but I didn't. But I will if you give me any trouble." Kingsley gave Tom a real close look at the gaping muzzles of the Baker 10 gauge.

Kingsley rolled Tom onto his stomach tying his hands behind his back, relishing the moans this caused. He pulled Tom's boots off throwing them across the small cabin. Standing, he lashed out and kicked the man savagely in the ass. "Get the hell up, boy."

Tom managed to find his feet, grinding the side of his face in the dirt floor of the cabin in the process. Once Tom was on his feet, Kingsley put the double barrel of his shotgun under his chin and barked. "Out that door and get mounted."

"I can't mount with my hands tied and no boots. And my arm's all shot up. You shot me, remember?" Tom said."

"I'll do worse than that unless you get your sorry ass in that saddle." Kingsley replied, pushing Tom out the door and toward his still-saddled bay horse. "Anybody leave a horse saddled overnight in this rain deserves what they get." He pushed him harder and Tom fell in the mud, Kingsley jerked him to his feet inciting a chorus of yelps.

"OK, I'm moving." Tom didn't have any idea how to mount a horse with his hands tied behind his back. He needn't have worried about it. When Tom reached his horse, Kingsley boosted him into the saddle effortlessly, like a man handling a child. The display of raw power destroyed the last vestige of hope in Tom.

Kingsley untied the reins and led the bay into the woods with Tom meekly slumped in the saddle.

The new day was overcast by angry gray clouds and the distant rumble of thunder. Last night's heavy rain had left the air crisp and sweet, but not to the poor wretch of a man astride that rain soaked horse. Every breath was a malodorous reminder that the end was coming. Tom Almer was staring death in the face and knew it, and there was nothing he could do about it.

Tom was about to meet his maker. The man leading his horse was the sorriest lawman ever to walk the face of the earth. Deputy U.S. Marshal Frank Kingsley heeded no judge or jury, followed no religious restraint, or contained even a shred of human compassion. Tom had heard Kingsley say on many occasions. "Kill 'em all and let the devil have his fill." Kingsley himself had lost count of the number of men he had killed. Killing had become a way of life.

Tom knew his life was over the instant he had seen Kingsley. It was only a matter of when. He had expected to die from that damned shotgun Kingsley carried around, but he hadn't and now he was on the back of a horse going god knows where and the longer he stayed alive, the more time he had to fan the flame of hope inside of him.

Kingsley hadn't killed Tom outright because he had something specific in mind for him. For the next hour, he led his mule and Tom's bay across the wet land until he came to the stage road. Taking it, he soon came upon what he was looking for.

The massive cottonwood tree had been growing here for over a century and sucked up plenty of water from the nearby Verde River. A smaller road used mainly by the locals intersected the stage road here. It headed almost due north along the Verde all the way to the Perkins Ranch and Sycamore Canyon. The stage road itself came from Jerome then continued east to Sycamore before turning south to Camp Verde. Anyone travelling either road passed this cottonwood tree.

Kingsley led the bay to a spot under a thick strong limb in plain sight of the road. He put a picket rope through the bridle and secured it to the tree, leaving enough slack for the horse to move about, but not enough to get far.

The tree was a favorite among the crows in the neighborhood and several thousand had gathered in the tree's massive canopy providing a very vocal audience to the drama below. A light sprinkle more mist then rain wet the land. Kingsley chewed a piece of dried goat jerky while going about his business.

"You kill Maggie?" Tom asked.

"What you think? You have got to be the dumbest Almer of the bunch. Your mother should have drown you at birth. Guess she left it up to me to do it for her." He munched more jerky as he pulled a second rope from the pack horse. He tied a hangman's noose in one end then threw it over the limb letting it hang about belt high on Tom.

"This ain't right King. None of it. You got no right to hang me. No right to kill Maggie. She didn't do nothing." Tom was becoming desperate. The hope he had nursed back to life was fading fast.

Kingsley tied the other end of the rope to the tree trunk, then slipped the noose over Tom's head and snugged it tight behind his ear.

"You can't do this. You're a lawman." Tom swallowed hard.

"Oh damn King, give me a drink. I know you always carry a bottle."

"I ain't wasting good whiskey on a dead man."

"Please, King... Have you no decency?"

Kingsley hunkered down, his back to the massive tree trunk looking up at Tom sitting on the back of the bay, his neck in the noose, bare foot without his hat. "None at all."

"We used to be friends King, good friends. I saved your life that time in Flagstaff. Remember?" Tom was cold and miserable and his arm was a constant pain, but he talked as if his life depended on it.

"Sure, I remember." Kingsley lit a cigarillo, cupping the stick match against the cold mist. The heat from the flaring match was warm to his hand. Taking a deep draw, he dropped the match on the wet ground. "And I surely do appreciate it." He smoked while Tom slumped in the saddle, unable to move, a noose around his neck, hope a thing of the past. Even the bay stood with his head down.

"Damn you King, you're enjoying this." Tom closed his eyes and muttered a prayer. "Lord, don't let him do this to me. He ain't got no right to hang me. It just ain't right. Lord, help me in this time of need."

His speech became erratic as fear overtook his thoughts. "Please god, don't let this happen. He can't do this. Lord, please don't let him hang me." He clenched his eyes tight shut and keep up a constant babble under his breath. Thunder rumbled in the far distance and the crows were a constant crescendo overhead.

All of this meant nothing to Kingsley. Without warning, he stubbed out his cigarillo on Almer's bare foot burning it badly.

Tom screamed and jerked his foot away spooking the horse beneath him. Reaching the end of his rope, eyes bugging out, he shut up.

Kingsley calmed the critter and moved the horse back under the limb. Tom gasped and sucked in air. "Just making sure you're awake for the hanging. It'll be your last. Wouldn't want you to miss it." He moved when Tom kicked out, just missing his head. "You got to do better than that, boy." Kingsley said. This was when he felt most alive, when he held another's life in his hands.

Kingsley relit his cigarillo, puffing on it until the tip was red-hot. He pulled smoke deep into his lungs and let it roll out his nose. His eyes grew wide with anticipation as he moved to the bay's hip, conscious of not getting kicked. A boisterous maniacal sound burst from his throat and he jabbed the animal hard in the rump with the hot tip.

"HEEYAAAAA..."

The horse leaped forward taking Tom Almer with him for a few feet. The sudden stop at the end of the hangman's rope snapped the outlaw's neck and left him wildly swinging under the tree.

"...*Ahhhhhh!*" What started out as a rebel yell turned into a cry of pure pleasure at the moment of death. The strange sound eerily echoes across the Verde Valley on this cold misty morning. The crows caw their approval as Tom swung back and forth beneath their perch. For almost a minute, Kingsley stood under that big cottonwood with eyes closed enjoying the kill.

Like a grandfather clock running down, the now limp body came to rest hanging under the tree. Kingsley casually checked that his mule was ready to travel. The misty rain had stopped again, so he removed his Fish slicker and rolled it tight, tying it behind his saddle. Kingsley took the deck of cards from his pocket, an old deck, well worn, the front a plain white. Finding the card he was looking for, he used Tom's knife to pin it to the trunk of the tree.

He stepped into the saddle. As he rode away, he rubbed the rain off his badge. Kingsley felt most alive after making a kill, and lately there had been many kills. Killing was his greatest joy, and doing it wearing a badge was even better.

Kingsley glanced back at the hanging body. "Two down. Four to go."

The crows made a ruckus as Deputy U.S. Marshal Frank Kingsley rode away. Behind him, a gust of wind gently swung the lifeless body of Tom Almer causing the wet rope to squeak on the tree branch, a sound lost among the chorus of bird calls.

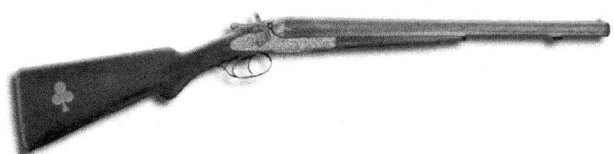

The four riders pulled up under the tree near the hanging body. Red Jack and the men had ridden hard. Their horses snorted in short bursts, lowering their heads with fatigue and standing with feet spread wide. Red Jack dismounted and turned the body to face him.

"Cut him down." He said.

Billy was beside him. "Shit, he killed Tom, oh shit..."

Red Jack backhanded him sharply. "Get hold of yourself."

"It had to be King. I'm going to kill that son of a bitch." Billy said holding the side of his head.

"We will, I promise you that." Red Jack said.

Yancy cut the rope at the tree trunk and eased the body to the muddy ground while Coulter retrieved Tom's bay horse. It was Yancy who found the card.

"You should see this." The breed was looking at something on the trunk of the tree.

Red Jack scowled and said. "What is it?" He went to look. "Jack of Clubs... Kingsley."

Yancy shrugged. "It's pointing that way." He pointed to the road.

"The son of a bitch is drawing us in." A chill ran down Red Jack's spine and he gave serious thought to running. It had been several years since the fiasco in Oklahoma forced him to leave in a hurry and it crossed his mind that now might be a good time to go back.

Billy looked at the card then at the road and asked. "What's up that way?"

"Sycamore." Red Jack said.

"Never been there." Billy said

"It's an old Mexican settlement near the Verde River. There's only about thirty white people and even fewer Mexicans. Farmers mostly, but there's a nice whore house and they got whiskey." Coulter said.

Yancy knelt beside the body and said. "Kingsley was here less than an hour ago." He pointed at Tom's bare foot. "He burned Tom."

"King tortured him? Why'd he do that?" Billy was horrified.

"Kingsley don't need a reason Billy. He's a force of nature."

Coulter replied.

"We bury him here?" Yancy asked.

Red Jack shook his head. "Ain't got time. We take him."

"Then where we going to bury Tom?" Billy asked.

"Sycamore, right alongside of Kingsley. Make sure you tie him on good." Red Jack had a strange foreboding that something terrible was about to happen. He told himself it was just nerves after losing Tom and Maggie so sudden like.

Yancy and Coulter draped the lifeless body on the back of the bay face down. They left the rope around his neck and used it to tie him to the horse.

When he was finished, Coulter reached into his saddlebag and pulled out a whiskey bottle. Taking a stiff drink, he handed it to Red Jack and asked. "Then we're going after Kingsley?" Seems Red Jack wasn't the only one having second thoughts about hunting the deputy.

"Damn right." Red Jack replied shoving aside any doubts he might have.

Lightening flashed and thunder rolled along the distant horizon as the four men started up the road towards Sycamore.

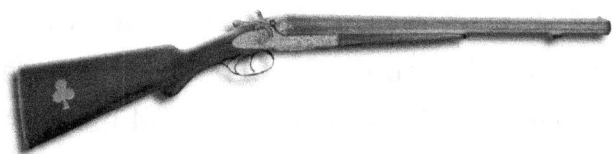

Tumbleweed Saloon's front porch was a popular place to pass the time in Sycamore. Some might say it was the only place to pass the time and they wouldn't be far off the mark. Today was no different. A local rancher, an old cowboy, the town's liveryman, and the bartender shared it this morning.

Hollister, a blue-haired Mississippi cowboy with one leg in a splint, was sitting in one chair with his busted leg resting on a second. "I tell you I can do the job." Hollister said. His homemade crutch, a piece of mesquite he had carved himself, was leaning on the porch rail close at hand. He had trusted a fresh broke horse a little too much and it had thrown him. That was four weeks ago. He had long since grown bored with town and wanted to get back to work.

Emmett Perkins, a lean man in his middle years, was owner and ramrod of the Pitchfork Ranch. His headquarters was a long rambling ranch house built of native adobe and stone a few miles upstream of Sycamore. He had picked a spot that gave him easy access to the Upper Verde River and a great view of Sycamore Canyon. Since he had been among the first settlers, the rancher considered the entire Verde Valley to be his and didn't like sodbusters coming in squatting on the best land. He had said once that he hoped lightning would strike every man dead that attempted to stick a plow into the ground.

"You got a broke leg and can't do the work. Relax and let it get better, then come talk to me." Emmett replied.

"He's got ya there." Quinn was standing at the edge of the porch near the top of the stairs. He looked up at the cloud cover then down the street towards the mercantile. "Sure is quiet. Like Sycamore's waiting for something to happen."

"Quinn, waitin's all we do around here." Hollister said, then turned to Emmett. "Mr. Perkins, I never said I couldn't work."

"Are you telling me you can? All of it?" Emmett looked sceptical. "Hollister, you sure as hell ain't getting any younger."

"Well, that's the gospel truth, none of us are." He looked to

Otis for support. Otis shrugged. As owner of the only Anglo saloon in town, he learned a long time ago not to take sides.

Emmett said. "Tell you what I'll do. I'll send one of the other hands to the north line shack…"

Hollister is grinning ear to ear. "Yes, sir... go on..."

"...to bring in those heifers and you can work with me at the ranch, long as you can keep up."

"Yes, sir, don't worry about that. I don't have a bum leg when I'm on the back of a horse or sitting a wagon seat."

"All right, ride out to the ranch and send Vernon to Oak Creek. Then, before daybreak tomorrow, hitch up the team and bring the buckboard back to town. I'll have the supplies waiting at the mercantile. Charles will help you load up and you take them back to the ranch. Luke can help you unload there. Think you can handle all that?" Luke was the ranch's cook and general homebody.

Hollister almost broke his neck nodding his head. "You bet, Emmett… er... ah... Mr. Perkins, damn, oh damn. Don't you worry. I can get it done. Thank you, sir."

Looking past Hollister, Quinn noticed movement at the far end of the street. "Someone's coming."

A man on a horse and leading a mule was riding into town.

Hollister leaned forward to see what had drawn Quinn's attention. "Who is it?"

Otis rose to his feet and stood by the porch rail gazing at the approaching figure. He whistled softly when he recognized who it was. "Damn my hide."

"What?"

"Coming this way."

Emmett turned to look. "Someone you know?"

Otis said. "I knew he would come back."

"Well, who is it?" Hollister said lurching to his feet, using the porch rail to lean upon.

"Kingsley. Frank Kingsley, that's who." Otis said.

Emmett got up from his rocking chair and moved to stand with the others. "Would that be the marshal with the scarred face? Thought he'd lost his badge."

Otis had turned pale. "Maybe he did, maybe he didn't, I don't know, but that's him riding up our street. And he's wearing a badge."

Quinn came to stand with them. "Yup, that's him all right. I was here in Sycamore back then, looked after his animal. That was before his scar. I've heard he's different now."

"How did he come by that scar?" Emmett asked.

Kingsley rode past the little gathering on the porch and stopped at the hitching rail outside the livery. He swung down and tied his horse then his mule. Both animals needed hay and grain, so he went inside to look for the liveryman.

"He took on the Mexican Army, what I heard." Quinn said.

"Lucky to be alive then." Emmett said.

"Sure, lucky is a word you could use. I wouldn't, but you could." Quinn said.

"Are you scared Quinn? He's a marshal. Why are you scared of him?" Emmett asked.

"You'll see." Quinn hurried down the steps and started across Main towards his livery. "You'll see."

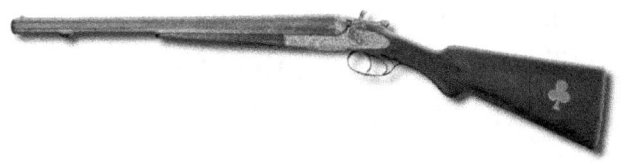

Billy Almer

Calling it a town was generous. The handful of buildings that was Sycamore lay among a stand of trees near the Verde River. The Sinagua and Hohokam had settled here first, long before the Apaches showed up. Mexicans came next. The Whites were the latest to settle here. Their wood and frame buildings were strung out along a single loosely defined street which they imaginatively called Main Street. It was the only street.

A giant cottonwood tree over a century old grew near the Verde River and roughly speaking, defined one end of Main Street, such as it was. At the other end was a small wooden bridge that passed over Mescal Gulch. It was here the tiny town divided itself with the Mexicans on the south downstream side and the Whites on the north.

Kingsley glanced at the hand painted sign at the edge of town as he rode past. There, in bright red letters, it read,

SYCAMORE, ARIZONA POPULATION ~~86~~ 87

From the deep shadow beneath his hat, his eyes took in everything. He had passed through Sycamore before, but that had been a while back. The large building next to the saloon hadn't been here then. It was unpainted board and bat construction with a large hand painted sign hanging across the front.

THE CHARLES HUDSON COMPANY

GENERAL MERCHANDISE & OVERLAND FREIGHT

Other smaller buildings were scattered along both sides of Main Street.

At the far end of town, the dense growth of old cottonwoods, scrub oak, and willows along Mescal Gulch formed a green wall broken only by the bridge. Beyond the bridge and close to the road was the two story adobe whorehouse. Its girls have been servicing local miners and cowboys for years and Kingsley knew it well. Beyond it and up hill lay more Mexican's adobe and stone buildings.

The marshal was also familiar with the local watering hole. The Tumbleweed Saloon was a two story wooden structure roughly in the middle of the little township and right next to the new mercantile. A wide, covered porch ran the width of the saloon across its front with a narrow alley separating the two buildings. Having only two windows in the front wall, and them overshadowed by the porch, light was hard to come by and burning lanterns was expensive so the inside of the saloon was rather drab and dim. More so on a day like today, overcast and stormy.

Kingsley walked up the saloon steps to the porch, his shotgun cradled comfortably, saddlebags over a shoulder. His face was unreadable and he moved with purpose. Cold brown eyes flicked over each man and settled on Otis.

"Evening marshal. I'm the barkeep. Let me know what I can get you." Otis said.

"Whisky." Kingsley said and went past Emmett, Hollister, and Otis to enter the saloon. Looking around, he made his way through the empty bar to a table near the potbelly stove and sat down in one of the rocking chairs that faced the front door.

The bar hadn't changed, it was how he remembered it. Running along the right wall, the bar itself consisted of several worn planks setting atop empty whiskey barrels. Behind it, right against the wall, was the back bar. On its shelves were bottles of whiskey and even some wine. It was the only piece of decent furniture in the whole place. The half-dozen tables scattered around the saloon were all handmade and the chairs around them an assortment with no two alike. High-backed chairs, low-backed chairs, stools and even a few rockers.

Otis followed Kingsley in and went behind the bar, grabbed a bottle, then stopped. Thinking better, he put it back and got another from the back bar. This was the good whiskey, only for special customers. He took the bottle and a shot glass and set them on the table in front of Kingsley.

"Obliged." Kingsley said.

The cast iron potbelly stove dominated the room, itself the center of a ring of more chairs This was the town's gathering place on many a cold day and night. On the wall opposite the bar, stairs led up to the second floor. The landing at the top had only one door leading to two rooms mainly used for storage, but Otis had a bed in one. Stacked beneath the stairs was a cord of seasoned firewood.

Emmett entered the saloon and went to retrieve the rifle he had left leaning against the bar. "Otis, I'll be on my way, but I'll see you tomorrow morning. I'll buy the marshal that drink." Emmett placed folding money on the bar, tipped his hat to Kingsley and moved toward the door.

Kingsley heard and poured himself a full shot glass. He then held it up to Emmett and said in his deep gravelly voice. "Obliged. May you beat the devil 'round the stump." He threw it down in one gulp gazing coldly at the rancher.

Emmett felt like someone had just stepped on his grave. He stopped at the door and looked back at Kingsley, tipped his hat once more and walked out, closing the door behind him. Nothing good was going to happen here today. Out on the porch, he called out. "Come on Hollister. We have work to do."

After Emmett had gone, Kingsley opened the Baker, popped out the two shells, standing them up on the table. He began wiping the gun down with an oily rag he pulled from his saddlebag. He took more shells from the saddlebag, carefully inspected each one, then stood them on end beside the first two. He loaded the shotgun laying it carefully on the table with its muzzle pointed towards the door. Then he pulled his pistol checking its load. With a sweeping motion, he smoothly spun the cylinder, bringing the gun to his ear, listening to its rhythm. Satisfied, Kingsley put the Colt back in its holster. He carefully placed the shotgun shells in his duster pocket in a way they could be quickly removed and loaded.

Kingsley found an old blanket laying on one of the chairs close to the stove and folded it neatly, laying it on his table next to the shotgun.

Otis picked up Emmett's money while keeping an eye on Kingsley as he inspected the weapons. He noticed the lawman always had one fully loaded gun close to hand while working on another. The lawman was getting ready for something and it wasn't a church social.

"Barkeep, bar the back door." Kingsley said. It wasn't a request and Otis never questioned why. It dropped in place with a thud.

Kingsley slid the table and rocking chair further behind the huge pot-bellied cast iron stove, putting it between him and the front door. He rested the double barrels of the Baker 10 gauge on the folded blanket, its muzzle pointed at the door. Only then did he pour another shot of whiskey, the rim of the bottle clicking once against the glass.

The thunder of approaching horses was loud on the muddy street. Otis moved to the window and looked out. "There's four of them."

Otis turned over a thick oak table and slid it in behind the bar and back in a corner forming a makeshift barricade. It was better than nothing against flying bullets. He was wishing he was some place else, any place, but here. Too late now.

Yancy, Coulter and the Almer brothers dismounted down the street on the far side of the mercantile. Red Jack checked his Colt Peacemaker one last time. "Watch this bastard. He's sneaky. He'll be in the saloon with that damn shotgun. Yancy, take the back. Billy, you take the outside stairs to the second floor. Me and Coulter will come through the front door. We'll flush the bastard out. Blow him all the way to hell where he belongs."

Without a word, Yancy led his horse around the mercantile towards the rear of the saloon. Red Jack untied the rope holding his dead brother to the bay. "Billy, give me a hand here."

They carried the body to a rickety high-backed chair among others sitting outside the livery and flopped it down. Red Jack wrapped the rope around Tom and the chair, pulling it tight. Rigor mortis had set in while he was on the horse. It caused his head and body to stay upright and his feet to jut out unnaturally.

Together, they lifted and carried the chair with Tom stiff as a board, setting him down in the street in front of the saloon. Red Jack snarled. "Billy, get up them stairs."

While they was doing that, Coulter found his spare pistol in his saddlebag. Checking it, he drew its twin from his holster and cocked both. He preferred Remington pistols to the Colt. And two guns are always better than one.

Red Jack waited until Billy was up the stairs, then shouted at the saloon. "KINGSLEY. WE KNOW YOU'RE IN THERE. COME ON OUT."

"Whisky's in here. Come on in, Jack, let me buy you a drink. We'll talk about it." Kingsley remained where he was with his shotgun cocked. The marshal's eyes never left the saloon front door. Staring down the length of the double-barreled shotgun, he patiently waited.

All sound faded away from Sycamore until a metallic click broke the silence.

Hearing the sound, Kingsley split his attention with the back door. The knob turned, ever so slowly, then someone pushed on the door, easy like. When the crossbar held the door fast, the knob turned back. It fell quiet once again.

A few seconds later, the front door opened a crack, a very small crack. Then, in an instant, it slammed wide open and Coulter came through, a pistol blazing in each hand.

Kingsley sat in the rocker, wearing his stone cold poker face, the wild light in his eyes the only indication he felt anything at all. Whatever he was feeling, fear was not part of it. As Coulter came through the saloon doors, Kingsley ignored the gunfire and simultaneously pulled both triggers of the Baker taking the man full in the chest with a twin load of double-ought buck. The lead shot not only stopped the outlaw cold, it blew him back out the door before he even crossed the threshold. Brute force drove his body across the porch and down the steps into the street, where it lay sprawled at the feet of a dead Tom Almer in his high-backed oak chair.

"*Ahhhhhh!*" Kingsley cried out but not in pain, with pleasure. When Otis peeked a look at him, the lawman had a wild eyed stare, his scared face twisted into an orgasmic sneer. "Never liked that son of a bitch." His tone was conversational, more that of a john talking with his whore.

Out on the porch, Red Jack Almer took one look at what was left of Al Coulter and started moving back towards the horses. Oklahoma was calling.

The back door rattled, hard this time. Kingsley shoved two more shells into the shotgun and surged out of the rocker. He fired point blank through the back door and reloaded before the spent shells hit the floor. The blast blew a melon sized hole through the planks above the security bar.

Kingsley pulled both hammers back to full cock and waited. Several rifle shots ripped through the door sending splinters flying and making the hole even larger. It also told Kingsley where the shots were coming from. The instant he caught movement through the hole, he pulled both triggers. A surprised yelp let him know he had hit someone.

A thump from above warned Kingsley to danger. He slid behind the bar with Otis where he could get a good angle on whoever was above him. He reached into his coat pocket for two more shells and shoved them into the shotgun.

From his position behind the table, Otis marveled at the coolness of the lawman. It was evident Kingsley had done this before and was enjoying himself.

Kingsley waited patiently, listening. The sound of a running horse came through the damaged back door. Seems Yancy was making a quick retreat or he wanted Kingsley to think it. He split his attention between the balcony above and the back door. His ears picked up the slightest sound. Not taking his eyes off the second floor landing, he laid the shotgun on the bar and pulled his pistol from its holster.

Moving to where he could watch the second story floorboards sag under the weight of the man, Kingsley fired two shots through the floor. He heard Billy curse. "*Damn!*" One of the bullets had creased his leg and sent splinters into his calf. Painful, but not life threatening. The door flew open on the landing and Billy fired down at Kingsley using the doorway as cover, but missed badly. Return fire drove Billy from the doorway. In desperation Billy retreated back into the room. Kingsley emptied his pistol through the floorboards as Billy ran and crashed through the upstairs window falling to the roof of the front porch, sliding down it, and dropping to the street with a thud.

By the time Kingsley made his way from behind the bar and through the front door, Billy was across the street and untying his horse. Kingsley ran to the edge of the porch. Billy fired, splintering the post close to Kingsley's head and forcing him to dive for cover.

Red Jack Almer had not yet fired a shot, but he had seen enough. This was a battle he could not win. He grabbed his horse, mounting it on the run.

Billy called to him. "Wait for me, Jack. Don't leave me." He grabbed the reins of his horse and painfully pulled himself into the saddle bleeding from several wounds. Something inside told him he wasn't going to make it.

Kingsley brought the Colt up, but the hammer fell on a spent shell as Red Jack Almer whipped his horse past in his bid to escape. Kingsley reached to his belt and pulled a single round from its loop shoving it into his pistol.

Mounted, but bleeding, Billy turned his horse intending to follow his brother. At that moment, Kingsley fired after Red Jack, hitting him in the thigh, not enough to knock him from the saddle, but it sure hurt like hellfire itself. Red Jack rode clear leaving his own brother behind.

Billy was hurting when he saw Kingsley shoot his brother. When the lawman began loading his pistol, he saw his opening. The boy outlaw kicked his horse out, heading straight at Kingsley, firing as he came. Billy was astonished at how fast the lawman loaded his gun.

Kingsley used both hands to fan the pistol, firing twice in quick succession. The two shots sounded almost as one.

Billy's horse went down flipping him headlong onto the street. The young man bounced and rolled, coming to a twisted heap at the lawman's feet.

The horse thrashed about and got up, limping away to stand in the middle of Main Street, glaring and snorting its dissatisfaction with recent events. Kingsley looked at the fast disappearing figure of Red Jack, then down at Billy and fired once more at the easy target at his feet. Billy's body jerked from the impact of the slug and the last bit of life left him.

"*Ahhhhhh!*" Kingsley cried out enjoying the kill. The lawman picked up Billy's pistol, then used the toe of his boot to flip the body face up. "Yep, he's dead." He then went to the limping horse and gently checked his foreleg. "You're all right. Come on."

He led the horse to the hitch rail in front of the saloon and tied him, then turned and took stock of his latest kills. How convenient. There was Tom Almer sitting in his chair, Coulter's bloody body at his feet, and Billy Almer all shot up. They was all right here as if they gathered here on their way to the bone orchard. Sheriff Garfias was right, people do die around him. In fact, maybe he should be charging the Arizona Territory per kill. Instead, all he gets is a lousy $100 a month. Hell, who's he kidding, he'd do this for free. And don't forget the other perks that come with the badge. He went down on one knee beside Coulter.

Mere moments after the shooting stopped, Otis came out on the porch and gawked at the dead bodies. From across Main, Quinn emerged from his livery and walked over. The brothers William and Charles Hudson came out of the mercantile to stare. Soon, the whole town would be there.

"Four out of six. Damn, Jack got away. Now I get to go hunting again." Kingsley said.

"Jack?" Otis asked.

"They're Red Jack Almer's bunch, or were." Kingsley replied.

"Red Jack Almer? Well, I'll be damned. Which one of them's Red Jack?" Quinn asked.

"He's the one that got away. This one is Al Coulter wanted in at least four states and two territories." Kingsley searched through Coulter's pockets and continued. "This back-shooting outlaw always had a hide out gun." He pulled back Coulter's rain slicker, revealing a deadly little Derringer in a shoulder holster. "Nice, huh?"

"Now, ain't that something? See that, Otis? See that? I bet he's killed a lot of innocent folks with that gun." As Kingsley pulled the shoulder holster loose from the body, Quinn continued. "Bet you've killed a lot of men, huh, Marshal Kingsley? You're the King."

Kingsley removed one of Coulter's boots. "I'm the law. I got a right to kill. Yeah, I got a right to do about anything I want. Guess that does make me the King. The King of Clubs."

Otis kept quiet, but not Quinn. He wasn't the brightest lantern in the barn. All he knew was that Kingsley was in a talkative mood so he dared ask him another question. "What's this one doing here? The one tied to the chair?" He walked over to take a closer look at the body.

"He's an Almer. I hung him early this morning." Kingsley finished cleaning out Coulter's pockets transferring the coin and paper money to his own then moved over to Billy Almer.

"This one's kind of young, ain't he?" Quinn said.

Kingsley didn't look up. "Old enough to wear a gun, old enough to die."

"I expect he's also some kind of kin to Red Jack?" Quinn asked.

"Brother."

Quinn nodded as if he thought so. "Red Jack Almer. Imagine that. Think he'll be back?"

"Not likely. He's a damn coward. Has to have somebody else do his killing. He just run out on his own brother and I killed his gun hands. Hell, he's run clean out of gun hands today." Kingsley was downright friendly.

Kingsley finished rifling through Billy's meager possessions and walked up the steps and into the saloon. He brought all the guns just collected from the dead outlaws and placed them on the bar with a clatter.

The two men followed, Otis taking his place behind the bar, Quinn staying close where he could see everything that went on.

"You got anything to eat?" Kingsley asked Otis. "Damned if I'm not hungry." He said cheerfully.

"Ah, sure. I got some fresh boiled eggs in pickle brine that might suit you, some bread and cheese." Otis could hardly believe it. Food was the last thing on his mind at the moment. He had just witnessed one of the bloodiest gunfights in his memory and the guy who done it was hungry? "I'm sorry Marshal Kingsley, cooking is not one of my talents."

"Whatever you have is fine. I'll let you know if I don't like it." Kingsley moved to the back door, removing the wooden bar from its cradle. Pulling open the badly mangled door, he said. "That damn breed also got away. He'll be halfway back to the Nations by now."

Kingsley went outside looking at the tracks and scuff marks

in the dirt. Over close to the mercantile, he found where Yancy had tied his horse. Several drops of blood meant he had hit him. How bad was unknown.

Returning to the saloon, Kingsley stepped up to the bar, poured a full shot and threw it back. "Where's the food?" It wasn't really a question, more of an accusation.

Otis went to the storeroom and brought back a plate of pickled eggs, a hunk of cheese and a half loaf of bread.

"You all got any law in this town?" Kingsley asked.

Quinn answered. "We got a few we try and live by..."

Otis cut him off. "Quinn, he means lawmen, like a sheriff." He looked back at Kingsley. "That was what you meant, wasn't it Marshal? We ain't got no sheriff."

Kingsley popped a whole egg in his mouth and chewed. "No law?" He chewed, swallowed, and asked. "Either you want these guns?"

Otis shook his head. "I ain't got no use for them." He already had a shotgun behind the bar, a pistol stashed in the back bar and two rifles upstairs. One of them the Enfield he used during the war.

Quinn's eyes lit up. "If you're giving them away, I'll take 'em."

"I ain't giving shit away." Kingsley took a huge bite of bread and cheese, chewing with his mouth open. Bits of food fell here and there, but he didn't notice or care. Taking another big bite, he chewed for a moment then asked Quinn. "You own the livery stable?" A speck of egg landed on Quinn's check.

"I do." Quinn said, brushing the egg away and moving down the bar away from Kingsley. He found it unsettling to watch this man eat as did most people.

Kingsley noticed the reaction then filled his mouth again. "Their horses." Food fragments splattered across the bar and onto the floor.

"I saw them." Quinn couldn't help himself, he watched Kingsley chew.

"You're buying 'em." A chunk of egg landed on the bar.

"They've been rode plumb into the ground." Quinn replied.

Kingsley popped another egg in his mouth. "Check them over. They'll come back. Fact is, that sorrel's a fine horse."

Quinn sensed that he was not going to win this haggle. "What you asking?"

"Fifteen a head, cash."

"That's what I can sell them for. I need to make something for my trouble." Quinn now felt he was in a box canyon with no way out.

"I ain't haggling. Fifteen a head. That's it." Kingsley's voice changed and Quinn nodded in agreement.

Kingsley took a bite of cheese and said, "Damn, that's good. Yeah, I sure do like your hospitality in Sycamore and the grub too. Eggs was just right."

Otis said. "They'll do."

Quinn asked. "You willing to throw in the saddles?"

"Tell you what, I'm feeling generous today. Fifty and everything is yours, the saddles, the guns, the works. All except the Derringer. I'm keeping that. That's my final offer, take it or... take it." Kingsley said, his tone turning hard.

Quinn couldn't agree fast enough. "Sure, sure, whatever you say Marshal Kingsley. Fifty for the lot is fine."

"What about burying all these bodies?" Otis asked.

Kingsley shook his head. "I just shoot 'em, I don't bury 'em."

Otis looked at Quinn. "You better get started with that fellow in the chair. He'll be stinking up the place before long."

Quinn was happy to change the subject. "Why am I suddenly in charge of burying?" Quinn asked.

Kingsley had his fill of eggs and was ready to leave. "My guess is you got the wagon. Now, pay up and I'll be on my way."

Quinn took out a leather billfold, counted out fifty dollars and held them out to Kingsley.

Kingsley took the money then grabbed the wallet. "Why is it you don't wear a gun?"

"Guns are dangerous." Quinn replied.

"Yes, they are." Opening the wallet, Kingsley took all the money and handed it back to the now terrified liveryman. "You weren't trying to cheat me, was you?"

"No sir." Quinn's hands shook as he put the empty billfold away.

"I didn't think so. Now if you'll excuse me, I'm going to go find me a whore." Kingsley said and walked out.

Quinn breathed a sigh of relief when the lawman was gone. "That man is the devil's own."

"And he looks like hell too." Otis replied.

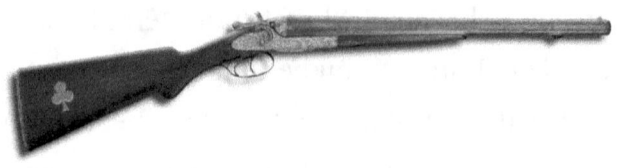

Jossy Banyon

ossy Banyon was in the barn, sitting on the stool, milking the cow. Beside her Lucretius, her cat, was begging for a bit of fresh cow's milk. One squirt, then another made her bite and gulp at the white stream with delight. Jossy laughed, enjoying the cat's antics. Taking care of the critters was one of the things she liked about living way out here.

Jossy had named the little Jersey cow, Buttercup and she milked her with the skill born of repetition. She had known the ways of a farm all of her young life, but found she wanted more. Now that she was married, other things, physical things, have come to her attention. She daydreamed about the night before when her husband Ben had been attentive to her. She became warm and wet just thinking about it. Growing up a farm girl, she was limited by a lack of sexual experience and dearth of anything approaching carnal knowledge. Her new husband didn't seem to have such problems.

Buttercup moved her back leg and almost stepped on Jossy's foot breaking into her thoughts. "Sooo boss. That's a girl."

The barn was one big room with a full loft above. There were two horse stalls and the milking stall had a stanchion along one wall. In the far corner was a tack room for saddles and harness. When Jossy finished milking, she released the stanchion that held Buttercup. Buttercup obediently backed out and walked to the far end of the barn as she did every morning waiting to be let out to pasture. Jossy let her out then carried the pail of milk toward the house with Lucretius and her kittens trailing along behind, meowing all the way.

Ben Banyon was shaving in front of the window taking advantage of the morning light. Hot water sat on the stove close at hand, a luxury he had grown fond of since moving here. Jossy was coming out of the barn heading for the house. He stared at his beautiful bride. How could he get this lucky? He sighed. He had never felt this way for anyone in his life. After what he had been through during the war, it scared him. He knew how fragile life truly was, how easily it can be taken. Fear of losing her was a pit eating away at his insides. He had never had anyone he loved this much. He felt vulnerable.

Being so thoroughly distracted, he nipped himself on the chin with his razor. "Damn." Ben muttered. He opened the door and reached for the milk bucket. Jossy smiled up at her husband and gently kept the cats outside with the toe of her work boot.

"It's finally stopped raining. Did you know you're bleeding?" Jossy asked.

Ben set the milk on the table and pressed on the cut with a finger. "As a matter of fact, yes." He moved back to the mirror to finish shaving, using a bit of warm water to rinse the blood off his face.

The main room of the house had a cast iron cooking stove

at one end and a stone fireplace at the other. In between was a large handmade table and a hutch filled with dishes. Right below one of two windows was a waist high floor cabinet with an oiled wood counter top. A single large cupboard hung on the wall back in the corner.

Across from the front door was the entrance to the master bedroom. Master because it had its own door to the privy out back. And last summer, right after their wedding, Ben had finished the loft turning it into a second bedroom. He had built a home for a family and everything was going as planned except for one thing, they had been married for almost a year and Jossy still wasn't pregnant. It wasn't for lack of trying.

Jossy went to the cupboard and retrieved a tin of baking soda. "Here, put this on that cut."

Ben took it. "Thanks. I'm thinking of letting my beard grow and stop this nonsense of shaving."

Jossy smiled and said. "Hush now, just put a pinch of this on it and it'll stop bleeding, but you've gotta hold it tight. Do that while I go change my dress. I'll only be a minute."

She sashayed into the bedroom, but was back in no time with scarcely anything on. Jossy smiled innocently up at her husband then turned her back wiggling her ass and jumping up and down as if having problems getting into her corset. Funny, she never had this problem before.

Flashing her enigmatic smile, Jossy backed up to him. "Ben, lace me up?"

Ben made a show of pulling her to him using the strings of the heavy garment, but all he did was make it fall to the floor.

"That's just great Ben. It'll be your fault if you're late

catching the stage." Jossy giggled standing nude before him.

"You let me worry about that." Ben picked her up and carried her into the bedroom leaving the corset on the kitchen floor. Laying her gently on the bed, Ben had his clothes off in seconds. His lips found hers then went on a tour of her body.

Jossy smiled down at him. "Take your time It's got to last me for a while."

His tongue found her sweet spot and she moaned, grabbing his head and pulling him even tighter to her. Hands stroked, fingers probed, and sweat glistened. Jossy found things to do with her mouth that she never dreamed possible before her marriage. Their bodies strained together as one. He entered her slow, feeling her accept him as he eased it in and out, each stroke penetrating deeper than the last. Having impaled her fully, the two young lovers found their rhythm. Instinctively, he worked to draw it out bringing them both to the edge, holding them there, then plunging them over.

"*Aahhhhh*." Ben called out as he deposited himself inside her then collapsed on top.

Jossy held him close. "I love you Ben Banyon, more than anything in the world." She said. "Hurry back to me."

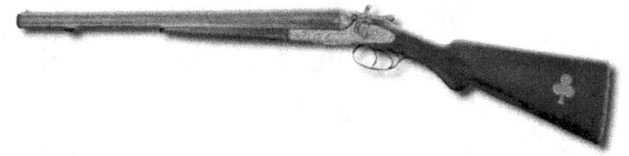

B en and Jossy huddled together on the buckboard's hard wooden bench seat enduring the cold drizzle. "Thought you said it'd stopped raining."

"It seems to have started again." Jossy said. "We can use it."

Thunder rolled across the sky above them and the horses found it hard pulling in the slick, wet Verde Valley mud. The Banyon farm wasn't far from town, but the going was slow this morning. The rain had stopped by the time they reached the little town at the edge of the Verde River. The occasional flash and rumble let them know the storm was still around.

Just as Ben and Jossy made the last turn, a lone rider came from town trailing a mule behind him. The brim of his hat was pulled low and the collar of his duster turned up hiding most everything. Only his face was partially exposed and that was in shadow.

The rider passed them on Jossy's side of the buckboard only a few feet from her. She glanced up just as a bolt of lightning sent stark shadows dancing across the most hideous face she had ever seen. She gasped loud enough for the man to hear. His eyes held hers for an instant, an image right out of a nightmare. It was an intense moment, something Jossy would never forget.

"*Hyaaaa*." Ben called out and snapping the reins, urging the team to better effort as soon as the rider had passed. He missed the entire exchange.

The front porch of the Tumbleweed Saloon was where local men would gather to talk of crops, the weather, or simply pass the time. This morning, Quinn, Hollister and Otis was there discussing the gunfight from the day before.

"Let me tell you. You ain't never seen anything like it. Cold as ice, Marshal Kingsley gunned down three of the toughest men in the Arizona Territory and sent two more running." While he talked, Quinn was whittling on the same piece of wood he'd been working on for two weeks. He leaned forward and spit a stream of tobacco juice all the way into the street. Otis had a broom and was sweeping the drying mud from the porch.

"Sorry I missed it." Hollister gulped down his second shot of whisky of the morning and stood up. Leaning heavily on his crutch, he hobbled off the porch and alongside the saloon where he proceeded to take a leak. The privy was too far for him to bother with.

The Banyon wagon approached and passed the saloon as sunlight broke through the clouds and began to take the damp chill from the air. Ben nodded a greeting to the men on the porch as he guided the team down the muddy street. Jossy still had her head covered with her rain slicker. She heard a man cough and looked to see who it was. It was Hollister taking a leak. She blushed and turned away. Ben didn't miss this exchange and glared at the man. Hollister grinned and, buttoned up his pants.

Banyon drove the team up close to the mercantile and climbed down. After helping Jossy down, he shook the water from his hat by slapping it upside his leg. Jossy wrung excess water from her hair, and caught Ben before he could tease her about catching Hollister making water.

"You so much as say one word to me, Ben Banyon, just one word and you'll be sorry."

"I didn't say a thing." He gave her the look and they both burst into laughter. Ben pulled her against him and gave her a kiss.

Quinn, Hollister and Otis watched from the saloon porch. "Ain't love grand." Quinn said.

Hollister grinned. "Naw, she caught me pissing. I think it got her all hot and bothered."

Otis stopped his sweeping and said. "Careful, she's his wife and trust me, Ben ain't someone to trifle with."

"No, I think he's right. She seen him all right, that's why they're laughing." Quinn said.

"Very funny. In a couple years she'll be all used up and worthless as a broke down mule." Hollister said.

"You horny old goat. You're the broke down old mule. Just look at you." Quinn said.

"I may be old, but I'm not dead. Don't look at me, look at her. That's one fine woman." Hollister rolled his eyes.

"How would you know what a fine woman looked like, Hollister?" Otis asked.

"I ain't always been here in this backwater."

"Humph, all I'm saying is watch your mouth. You always get a bad case of dumb ass when you're drinking." Otis finished sweeping and went back into the saloon, leaving Hollister and Quinn to swap lies.

"What's up his craw?" Hollister asked.

Quinn looked at him. "Ain't you been listening? There was a shoot out in his saloon yesterday."

Inside the saloon, a group of farmers were gathered around the huge pot-bellied stove talking and smoking. Two of them were Karl Fortenberry and Angus Campbell. Fortenberry was a German immigrant and hard working man who was always looking for an angle, a user. Angus was a different sort of person, a deliberate thoughtful man content in finding ways to improve everyone's lot in life, a borrower.

Sitting alone at a nearby table was a young gunhand, Warren Neally. He was playing an endless game of solitaire and waiting.

He had arrived that morning just after daylight and banged on the door of the saloon until Otis had finally let him in. No one knew what he was waiting for which made them all a little skittish.

Otis called to the farmers as he went behind the bar. "Looks like it's stopped raining and Ben just drove up to Hudson's Mercantile."

Angus dallied while the other farmers put on their coats and shuffled out of the saloon. The sudden out flow of people forced Hollister to wait outside until they cleared the door. When he did step in, he almost ran into Fortenberry. The two men glared at each other until Fortenberry pushed past him calling over his shoulder. "Angus, you coming?"

"Aye, in a moment."

Hollister scowled at Fortenberry's back then went to the bar sitting his shot glass on it. "Pour some whiskey in this. I need a drink with all these squatters hanging 'round."

Otis reached behind him for a bottle. "More whiskey ain't going to make it better." He poured the glass full.

Hollister laid a coin down on the bar and took a gulp. A second and third emptied the glass. "MMMmmm... Damn, do it again. That hit the spot."

"You sure?"

"Hell yes. I asked, didn't I?" Hollister laid another coin down as Otis poured. This time he sipped the whiskey. "That should do me for a spell."

"You got that right. Any more and Emmett will get on me for getting you drunk." Otis said.

"Don't you fret none 'bout that." He turned to look at Angus. "You know, Otis, too many damn squatters moving in. Someday we're goin' to do something 'bout it, you'll see." Hollister was already deep into the whiskey.

"You talk too much." Otis said."

"One of these days, you know what I mean. Clean out the squatters." Hollister gulped down more whisky.

The young gunfighter glanced up from his game, listening, watching. He sized up Angus as he moved past Hollister who was now standing with his back to the bar.

"You don't know what you're talking about, Hollister." Angus said in his English accent.

Hollister grinned. "I'm talkin' 'bout cleanin' up the territory. Gettin' rid of the vermin."

Otis slapped the bar hard with the flat of his hand. "***Hollister.*** What did I tell you? Watch your mouth."

Hollister jumped at the sudden sound behind him. "Well shit, it's true, ain't it? Why shouldn't I tell the truth?"

"Let it be." Otis warned his friend again.

"Farmers have just as much right to be here as anybody. This isn't the old country where the king makes all the rules. This is America, the land of the free." Even though Angus was born and rased in Edinburgh Scotland, he spoke with a British accent having learned the King's English in some of the finest schools the British Empire had to offer. He considered himself an educated man. Seeking a new life, Angus had come to Arizona by wagon train along the southern route and after getting married, the newlyweds listened to the stories and decided to settle in the Verde Valley. None of that mattered now.

Hollister looked hard at Angus. "Sodbuster, I don't know what you just said. You speakin' English?" Then he dismissed him with a drunken laugh. "Never could cotton to foreigners. They should all just go back where they came from."

Angus was a tall man with plenty of muscle, but a sense of morality that precluded violence. He used every bit of it to keep himself from smashing the face of this ignorant drunk. He could take a dozen sober Hollisters and turn them into blood pudding without breaking a sweat, but he didn't work that way. Angus was a gentle giant and Hollister knew that from previous run-ins with the man. He had never felt threatened and now believed he could say anything to him without fear of reprisal. He was right, mostly.

Angus never said a word, just set his coffee cup down on the bar and turned for the door. The gunfighter shoved an empty chair in front of him, blocking his path. "That was downright cowardly. You a coward, plow boy? Is that why you let this cowboy talk to you that way?"

Angus stopped and swallowed hard. Everyone in town knew Neally was a gunfighter, they had about five minutes after he arrived. Angus never turned, never looked at him, he just said. "The man has no right to threaten me, my family or my friends. We have as much right to the land as Perkins or any other rancher."

"Only if you can hold it." Neally said. "Can you hold it sodbuster? You're wearing a gun, but from what I seen here, you're a damn coward."

Angus twitched then knocked the chair from his path with a flick of his hand.

Neally surged to his feet ready to draw.

Otis leaned across the bar aiming his double barreled shotgun straight at Neally. "Don't move mister, less you think you're faster than this morning's lightning. Don't move one hair."

Neally snarled. "Barkeep, this ain't your fight.

"Angus is a friend and this is my bar. If anybody is going to die here, it will not be him."

Neally relaxed and moved his hand away from his pistol. "I don't like folks waving guns in my direction."

Otis said. "Oh you needn't worry about that. I ain't waving shit. I got a right steady finger on both triggers."

Neally took a deep breath, and sat back down in his chair. "Looks like it's your lucky day, plow boy."

"This stranger's got some kind of excuse, but Angus, you and Hollister are being just plain stupid." Otis said. So much for not taking sides.

"I'm stupid? Someone needs to teach Hollister civilized manners." Angus said.

Hollister took another gulp of whiskey. "I know all 'bout manners, thank you very much. You ain't teaching me shit." He was feeling no pain and wasn't even fully aware of what was happening at that point.

"Undoubtedly." Angus said. "This has gone far enough." He walked out of the saloon.

Otis kept his eyes and gun on Neally until the farmer had gone.

"You going to keep that scatter gun on me all day?" Neally asked.

"Just being cautious." Otis released the hammers on the shotgun and returned it to it's place under the bar, leaned up between two barrels. He reached for a new bottle of whiskey, took it to the gunfighter's table and poured a glass. "On the house."

"Obliged." the young gunhand dealt himself cards. As Otis was walking away. "Barkeep, if you ever pull that gun on me again, I'll put a bullet in you."

"Then we understand each other." Otis replied returning behind his bar. If he ever again pulled the shotgun on this arrogant young man, he would kill him.

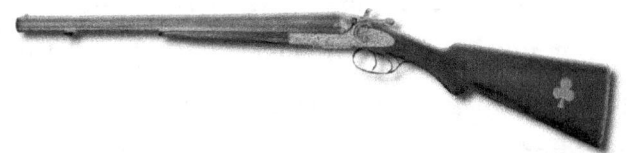

B en, Fortenberry and the other farmers stood in front of the mercantile talking when Angus came out of the saloon. Standing apart from the men, Jossy was also in front of the mercantile brushing out her wet hair. Angus clumped down the boardwalk towards her.

She looked up. "Hello, Angus." She went back to brushing her hair.

Angus tipped his hat. "Good morning, lass."

Jossy looked up at him again. Only then did she notice his expression, he looked like he just buried his favorite dog. Not wanting to poke into another's business, she went with the weather. "Turned out to be quite a storm. Wetter than we was expecting."

"Aye, that it was." Angus said.

She hadn't known the man long, but Angus wasn't usually this serious. Jossy sensed that something was wrong, but instead of being direct, she kept up the small talk. "What is it you're always saying about predicting the weather?"

"You mean, only fools and newcomers do it?" The big man responded.

"Yeah, that's it. I qualify for both."

Angus frowned and shook his head. "Oh, no, lass. You're neither."

"You're too kind, Angus. You're also too late. The word is already out, this newcomer is a fool." She grinned up at him.

Angus would have none of it. "You may qualify as a newcomer, but you're no fool, lass." He stood there looking down at her and felt his blood rise to his face realizing he was talking to a woman he only barely knew in a place he never knew existed a few short months ago. "Please excuse me, I must be going." He stammered and made his escape towards the other men. Jossy could do that to a worldly man which Angus was not. He's always had trouble with pretty women, even worse before he was married. Strangely enough, the encounter with Jossy made him feel better, especially after what went on in the saloon just now. Simply being near her changed him.

Angus thought again about hanging his gun up for good, stop wearing it. Other men have done it and lived. He was coming to the conclusion that wearing a gun was far more dangerous than not wearing a gun. At least for him personally. The thought of drawing the gun and killing another human being left him cold inside. He didn't think he could do it.

As Angus walked up, Fortenberry was saying to Ben and the other farmers. "If it was up to me, Ben, I'd say sure thing, let's give it a try. But you know, it ain't just me I got to think about. If there's trouble and something happens to me, who's going to take care of my family?"

"I understand. Oh, howdy, Angus." Ben said.

"Ben." Angus said.

"Fortenberry says he's not sure he wants to stick it out."

Angus shrugged. "Can't say as I blame him. Some of the folks in this town are not very friendly."

Ben looked at Angus. "Doesn't mean you give up. Anything worth having is worth fighting for. I ain't giving up."

"Then you're still going?" Fortenberry asked

"I am." Ben glanced at Jossy standing apart from the men. "Just waiting on the stage. If you want me to buy for you, I can."

"Angus, you planning to stick around?" Fortenberry asked.

"Aye, I stand with Ben. To build anything worthwhile needs effort and commitment. This valley can grow crops, and I expect the Verde to have water year round. We can build something here that will last. This is what I want for my family." Angus said.

Others nodded in agreement. Ben smiled. "Good, glad to hear it."

Angus shrugged his broad shoulders. "I've got some other ideas. I've looked at the Verde upstream of us and think we could build ditches to bring water to our fields. The Indians done it years ago and we can follow what they did. The remains of a large and very old Indian settlement are nearby, and other ancient ruins of a long occupation are all around us, caches and shelters built into every nook and cranny."

"What could those savages know about farming?" Fortenberry asked suspiciously.

"Those *savages* irrigated fields for miles up and down the

river. They must have known something." Angus replied. There was something about Fortenberry that Angus didn't like or maybe he found prejudice revolting wherever he found it.

Ben was pleasantly surprised. He was coming to depend on this bear of a man for many things, more today than most. "Show me what you have in mind when I get back. Right now, the mercantile's got a new seed catalogue to show everyone. Let's step inside and decide what we all want."

Ben lagged back as the other men went inside. Jossy came and slid smoothly into his arms looking up at him. "I'm so proud of you. Never thought it possible, but I love you more every day. I just wish..." Her voice trailed off.

"Quit that, you hear? What will happen will happen and that's it. No use fretting about stuff we can't change. I will love you, kids or no kids."

Jossy smiled warmly. "You better, Ben Banyon. I don't know what I would do with you if you didn't."

Angus said from the door of the mercantile. "I hate to interrupt, but the stage is due in any time. Let's have a look at that catalogue."

Jossy grinned and reluctantly released her husband. Continuing to brush out her hair, she drifted to the edge of the porch. A lone rider appeared at the far end of town beyond the livery corral. It was that rancher, Emmett Perkins.

Jossy watched Emmett approach with growing trepidation. The rancher had said some things against the farmers in the past and she trusted him about as far as she could throw him. He certainly had the most to lose. As Emmett tied his horse in front of the saloon, a skinny kid she didn't know emerged, a drink in his hand and his gun tied low on his leg. Hollister tagged along behind. They didn't see Jossy right away.

"Hey boss." Hollister said.

"Where are we with the supplies?" Emmett asked, his boots thudded heavily upon the steps leading up to the porch.

"The wagon's being loaded right now. Should be ready in 'bout an hour."

"Good." Emmett nodded. He could smell the whisky.

The kid nudged Hollister. "Oh, boss, this is... What did you say your name was?"

"Warren. Warren Neally. Very glad to make your acquaintance, Mr. Perkins. I'm looking for a job if you have need of a hand good with a gun and a rope."

Emmett looked him over. "Where are you from?"

"Austin, Texas."

"What did you do there?"

"Punched cows mostly." Neally had mostly tended the needs of the local ranchers, everything from mowing hay to slopping hogs. Anything for a sawbuck. That all changed the moment he strapped on the Colt Peacemaker. It had been his father's. That gun was the only possession he had that meant anything to him. From the first time he held it in his hand, it felt like an extension of his arm. Speed and accuracy came natural. The morality in which to use his gift was quite another thing entirely.

"Why did you leave?"

"I outdrew the mayor's son and busted up his shoulder. After the fight, he couldn't whack his own johnson let alone draw a gun again." Neally had shot the man before he touched his gun, before he even knew he was in a gunfight.

"So you thought it best to leave town?"

Neally grinned coolly, arrogantly. "I thought it best to leave Texas, sir." If he hadn't, Marshal Ben Thompson would have hung him for sure.

That's when Hollister noticed Jossy a short space away on the mercantile front porch. "Morning Mrs. Banyon. Seen anything interesting lately?" He smiled drunkenly.

Jossy blushed, but didn't say anything, ignoring him.

When Neally saw Jossy, he held his glass up in a toast, letting his eyes appreciate her curves and porcelain skin.

Jossy felt like one of his saloon girls and didn't like it. She turned on her heels and walked into the mercantile shutting the door behind her.

Hollister and Neally both laughed.

Emmett's eyes narrowed. "I'll let you know if I need someone, Mr. Neally. Hollister, you best get your ass over to that wagon and make sure its loaded proper. Now if you'll excuse me." Emmett crossed the porch and entered the saloon.

Neally remained standing looking after the rancher. He turned to Hollister. "What's that mean? You said he could use a hand. Was you lying?"

Hollister held up his free hand. "No sir, I wasn't lying. It just takes a bit for Mr. Perkins to warm up to a body. Give him time." Hollister cocked his head recognizing the sound of an approaching stage. The sound grew until it filled the still morning to overflowing. Opening the saloon door Hollister called out quite unnecessarily. "Here comes the stage, Mr. Perkins."

The driver, an older man with a full gray beard, had his hands full with the six horses. The stage barreled down the street past the saloon. *"**Whoa, Whoa, damn it, Whoa!**"* It pulled to a muddy stop in front of the mercantile which doubled as the depot and post office. Several hands were waiting to replace the team with a fresh one for the stage's journey up Cleopatra Hill to Jerome. The driver looked down at the farmers and townspeople that had come out to welcome the stage and collect any mail or merchandise he carried. He said. "Howdy folks. Whoever's planning to ride with me, be ready to go as soon as the fresh horses are hitched." He climbed down with the mail pouch and went into the mercantile. Several followed him in.

Emmett came out of the saloon, clumping down the boardwalk towards the mercantile. The stage hands were busy hooking up the fresh team, and that sodbuster, Banyon and his woman were on the boardwalk in front of the mercantile watching them work. The woman fussed with his tie.

"Hold still." Jossy said.

"I am holding still. Look, I don't like this anymore than you do, but I would feel better if you were with Angus and Mary while I'm away."

"I'll be fine. Stop worrying." Jossy said.

"I will worry, Jossy and as you can tell, I'm not any good at pretending to not worry, especially when I'm worried."

"I love you, Ben Banyon."

He pulled her close and gave her a kiss. "We won't be doing this much, me going off without you."

She looked up at him, "Promise?"

Emmett cleared his throat as he walked up. Ben gave him his attention. "Can I help you Mr. Perkins?"

"I doubt it." Emmett moved around them and climbed up on

the stage. He looked under the driver's seat, in the boot, and had started rummaging through the cargo on top when the stage driver came out the mercantile.

"You looking for something in particular?" The driver asked.

"Yeah, a new rifle."

"Well, if your name is Emmett Perkins, then I got something for you. You'll find it wrapped in a blanket under the back seat. Yes, sir, I was keeping it safe."

Emmett opened the stage door and pushed up the back seat, lifting out a long woolen blanket. He smiled as he unwrapped the brand new Winchester 73. He worked the lever, bringing the rifle up to his ear listening and feeling the smooth action. The look on his face was pure pleasure. "Much obliged." He headed inside the mercantile to buy ammunition for his newest rifle.

Ben put his arm around Jossy drawing her away from Emmett to let the rancher pass. Emmett politely touched his hat on the way by. "Ma'am."

The driver climbed up on the stage and Ben tossed his carpetbag up to him. Jossy whispered something to Ben that made his ears turn red and he said. "I'd sure feel better if you'd go stay with Angus and Mary."

"Now, Ben, I thought we had all that settled. I have lots of things I'll be able to catch up on with you not underfoot. You don't leave me alone long enough to get anything done." She smiled mischievously.

Ben feigned shock. "Jossy Banyon, you're nothing, but a fallen angel."

"Only when I'm around you." Jossy pouted. "Now go buy your seed and hurry back to me."

Angus came out of the mercantile followed by several of the others and walked over to Ben and Jossy. "My good man, we even got Fortenberry to buy seed. You have a full list. I only hope you can get it all in one wagon." Angus said handing full wallet and a folded piece of paper to Ben.

Ben slipped the wallet into an inside pocket and opened the paper running his eyes down the list. "Almost nine ton. Good. If I need two wagons, then I will hire two wagons."

Angus made note of how fast Ben absorbed the information on it. It was another sign that there was more to his friend than most would suspect.

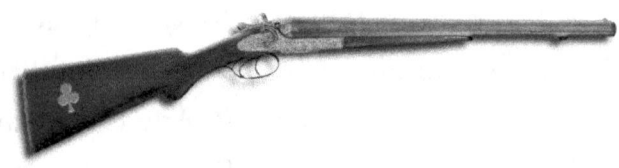

Warren Neally

Neally had watched the whole scene from the saloon porch and decided to make his play. If Mr. Perkins needed some encouragement to hire him, he knew just the thing to do.

The gunman made his way down the boardwalk to the group of farmers outside the depot. They seen him coming and parted like the Red Sea.

But instead of passing them, Neally stopped and stared at Angus towering over the other farmers. "You there, the big coward. Get your ass over here."

Angus frowned. "What do you want, sir?"

"I want you out of town, now. Not later, right now. I plan on doing some drinking and your stench is making me sick."

Angus remained still while the other farmers moved away from him. He now faced Neally across an open boardwalk. " I do not want to play this game."

Neally laughed coldly. "This isn't a game, sodbuster. One of us ain't walking away and it's not me." His hand hovered over his pistol. "I ain't never killed anybody as big as you before."

He had only wounded three men, none in a stand up fight. This would be his first actual kill. His heart was racing and blood pounded in his ears.

Ben moved Jossy into the mercantile out of the line of fire as the others scrambled to do the same. The porch was suddenly very empty.

"I'm going to kill you sodbuster, right here in front of your stinkin' sodbustin' friends. You ready to die?"

Ben stepped up beside Angus and moved his long coattail, clearing his holster. "The real question is, are you ready to die? Can't get both of us. You make a move and one of us is going to get you."

Neally snorted. "You don't think I can take two sodbusters?" His right hand hovered above the gun on his hip. "I'll even let you make the first move. Go on, damn it, one of you draw."

"You need to find yourself something better to do with your time, young man." Emmett had returned, seeing what was happening outside the mercantile. "I will not hire you if you gun down any of these people. That's not how I do business."

This gave Neally pause. "This is my fight, Mr. Perkins. Not yours." But it distracted him and he was suddenly unsure of himself.

That's all it took. Angus crossed the boardwalk in several quick steps and backhanded Neally so hard he flew off it landing in a heap on the street. The stage horses whinnied and stomped, nervous at what was going on so close by.

Angus jumped off the porch and pulled the man's pistol from its holster tossing it further out into the muddy street. The big farmer jerked the gunman to his feet and backhanded him again then shook him like a child with a rag doll.

Emmett came and laid a hand on the big man's arm. "That's enough. I think he got the message." Turning to the other farmers. "Y'all know I don't take to killing. I won't tolerate it. Never have."

He reached down and picked up the fancy engraved pistol out of the mud, emptying its cartridges onto the street. "Where's your horse?"

Neally spit blood then nodded towards the hitch rail in front of the saloon. He wiped his bleeding nose with a shirt sleeve looking dazed and confused and more than a little angry. Emmett called out. "Hollister, bring Mr. Neally his horse. The feller is leaving town."

Hollister stepped lively, and led Neally's horse over to his boss. Hollister held the reins and then handed them to Neally after he mounted. Emmett looked up at him. "Young feller, you're getting out of here with your life. Be smart and never come back to Sycamore."

The rancher pulled the trigger of his new rifle firing it up in the air and slapped the flank of the horse at the same instant. *"Now get."*

The horse reared forcing Neally to grab hold of the saddle horn or get thrown for sure. As the horse raced out of town, Hollister yelled out. "AND DON'T EVER COME BACK."

"Thought I told you to tend the wagon?" Emmett said.

"Was on my way." Hollister said heading towards the mercantile.

Jossy emerged from the mercantile and rushed at him, throwing herself in his arms. Ben braced himself just in time,

"You could have been killed." Jossy was scared.

Ben shook his head and grinned. He rather liked having someone worry over him. "Things are fine."

Jossy was having none of it. Now she was angry. "What do you mean risking your life like that? Damn it Ben." She wanted to knock some sense into her man, but instead found herself hugging him so tight he groaned.

Ben shook his head again. "Not in public." He whispered in her ear.

Jossy let him go and looked up at him. "Ben, I need you beside me, not in the ground somewhere."

"She's right lad, You shouldn't have stepped in." Angus said.

"And just let you get shot? I don't think so. Is that what you would have me do, Jossy? Watch a friend get shot down? I did too much of that during the war." He stopped when he realized what he had said. He hated talking about the war. The stage driver saved him.

"ALL ABOARD. We're running late and need to make up lost time. ALL ABOARD. *Let's go folks.*"

Ben turned to Angus. "See that Jossy gets home all right."

"Just as we agreed, lad. You know that. Mary and I will take good care of her. Now, climb in before you get left behind."

Jossy was still mad, but she was dying to hear more about the war. Ben had told her so little of what had happened to him. She's sure he had left out most of it.

Ben tried to give her one last kiss, but she turned her face away. He shrugged and climbed into the stage.

Jossy relented, not wanting that to be the last thing she remembered of Ben until his return. She leaped onto the coach's step. The two kissed through the open window and she jumped down as the driver gathered up the lines and flipped them against the horse's backs. The driver yelled at the top if his lungs. "YEHHHHHUUUU" The horses lunged into the collars, their hooves digging into the mud. As it made the turn at the edge of town, Ben looked back at his lovely wife and waved one last time. He told himself for the millionth time, this was necessary and everything would be fine.

Jossy stood and looked after the stage until it was out of sight. Angus helped her through the mud to her wagon. Jossy took up the lines as Angus tied his own horse to the back of the wagon and climbing in beside her.

"Don't fret, lass. He will be back before you know it." Angus said taking the reins from her.

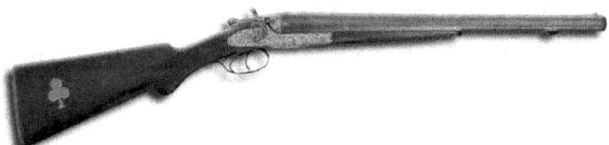

As day turned into night, lamp light spilled out the open front windows and door of the house, thrown wide to catch the slightest breeze. Jossy had been busy all day, cleaning and arranging things that she hadn't taken time to do before. She loved putting her own house in order. Dinner with the Campbells was a fine finish to a grand day.

Angus Campbell, followed by his wife Mary, carried two chairs out of the house and placed them where they would find the slightest movement in the hot still air outside. After a good rain storm, the air in Verde Valley stayed humid and heavy for days.

Jossy emerged carrying her own chair and the rifle which she leaned up against the house close to hand.

"Here, let me get that for you Jossy." Angus said making a move towards her.

Jossy laughed and said. "If I can't carry my own chair then grab a shovel, I need burying. Sit down and enjoy the evening. Tell him Mary. Women don't need men around near as much as you think."

Mary laughed. "I wouldn't go that far, Jossy. They are handy for some things." She patted her belly, her pregnancy not yet showing. The expression that flashed across Jossy's face made Mary regret her comment as soon as it was out her mouth.

"You're sure you're with child?" Jossy asked.

Mary nodded. "A woman knows."

Looking distinctly uncomfortable, Angus sat down in his chair which creaked ominously under his weight. He fidgeted for a moment then stood. "I think I'll get the team hitched." He was down the steps and heading across the yard to the barn before either woman could say a word. They could see the big man's blond hair bob about even after he was in deep shadow within the barn.

Mary giggled like a little girl. "I just love that man."

Jossy looked quizzically at Mary. "Should I take it personal?"

Mary shook her head. "Heaven's no. In fact, I never seen him sit down at another woman's table... *ever*. You folks are the only visiting we have done since we moved here six months ago. Quite the opposite, Angus likes you and your husband. He thinks Ben is a fine man."

Jossy felt a surge of pride. "On that we agree."

"When do you expect him back?" Mary asked.

"Tomorrow night at the earliest. Could be a couple days though. Hard to say for sure."

"And it doesn't scare you to be out here by yourself?" Mary asked.

Jossy didn't laugh. "A little, but I have you and Angus just a mile away and I keep the rifle close by."

Mary reached over and squeezed Jossy's hand. "You call on us any time, night or day."

Jossy nodded. "Ben said you can hear the rifle from your place. You think so?"

Mary frowned and looked to the south. "Maybe... Ask Angus, he would know for sure. He has some fancy schoolin' from over in England."

"He has a wonderful British accent. I could listen to it all day. How did you two meet, if you don't mind my asking?" Jossy leaned forward to see Mary's face in the moonlight.

Mary looked slightly embarrassed. "Oh, well... It was at a social put on by the wagon master. I made a nice apple pie that he liked, but he wouldn't come over and tell it to me. Instead he stood where he could see me and stared. Almost didn't happen because he's so shy."

"What did you do? Come on Mary. I know you well enough to know you didn't just sit on your hands and wait for him." Jossy raised her eyebrows expectantly.

Mary smiled at that. "No, I didn't wait for him. I found out who he was and which wagon was his and I made up some cockamamy story about needing help moving a trunk. It worked though. Once I got him talking, I couldn't shut him up. We was married in Albuquerque about a month later."

Jossy laughed. "I look forward to that day, when Angus will talk my ear off."

"I heard my name. What are you telling her, Mary?" Angus had the team hitched to the buckboard and was walking them across the yard to the house where he tied them to the rail.

"Nothing, but the truth, so help me god. She asked if we would hear a rifle shot from our place? What do you think?" Mary asked.

The big Scotsman rubbed his chin, turning to look south. "Aye, a ghrá mo chroí, maybe, but I doubt it. And if we did hear it, would be hard to tell which direction it was coming from at that distance. Sound makes funny bounces off the hills, but if you were to try, be sure to be outside and fire three quick shots. I would be here before the rifle cooled."

Jossy smiled. "Thank you both so much, but if you hear three shots, it's because someone needs burying and I don't want you to come rushing in here and get yourself killed too. I can handle myself."

Angus nodded. "Lass, I'm sure you can, but just the same, I will keep an ear open. Now, come mother, it's time for us to go home."

The stark change in expression at the mere mention of mother motivated Mary to go to Jossy and the two women hugged. Mary whispered in Jossy's ear. "You will have yours, don't worry. They will come."

"I know." Jossy smiled, but her heart wasn't in it. She watched after them until the buckboard disappeared around the bend.

She went inside and cleaned up the dinner dishes putting them away. Reluctantly, she made sure the front door was latched and the windows all closed and locked. It would get very stuffy inside the house by morning, but she had no choice. She blew out all, but one coal oil lamp which she took into the bedroom with her. She removed her dress and underclothes and slipped on a full length robe, tying the sash about her waist. Blowing out the lamp, she lay down on top of the covers. She has grown accustomed to having Ben's warm body next to hers and only now did it fully hit her how much she missed him. After what seemed like half the night, she dropped into a fitful sleep.

Hours later, Jossy stirred when she felt Lucretius jump up on the bed. She opened her eyes. "What are you doing in here?" Jossy swung her legs out of bed and Lucretius rubbed against her. "Come on. Let's put you out. Your babies need their momma." She went to the dresser, stuck a match and lit the coal oil lamp keeping its light low.

Coming out of the bedroom, she sat the lamp on the table. With Lucretius following right along, she unlatched and started to open the front door. Before she knew that anything was wrong, someone kicked the door wide open throwing her back against the table.

Jossy cried out, but didn't wait around to see who it was. She scrambled for the rifle leaning up against the wall just inside the bedroom door. Jossy was fast, but the man was faster. He knocked her down and landed on her chest pinning her to the floor.

Lying flat on her back, Jossy looked up into the man's face as he leered down at her. "Hi, little lady. Remember me?"

It was that young gunfighter from town, Neally.

"What do you want?" Jossy asked.

Neally laughed. "What do I want? Isn't it obvious what I want? I want you."

Neally grabbed up the rifle and worked the lever until it was empty then tossed it aside. Still sitting on Jossy, he reached down and ripped her robe open revealing her bare breasts. Just staring at them sent waves of lust washing over him so that he didn't notice Jossy grab her shears from her sewing basket sitting on the floor close by. She struck him a glancing blow cutting through his shirt and slicing his shoulder drawing blood. He cried out in pain. "YOU DIRTY BITCH."

He grabbed her wrist before she could swing again. Skinny as he was, his dead weight on her chest was too much for Jossy to overcome. From his advantage atop the young woman, he bent her arm over his leg. "I'll break it, bitch! Drop it." He applied pressure until she released the shears. Neally knocked them across the room out of reach, turning back just in time for her to spit in his face.

"Now that's more like it." He snarled at Jossy, then wiped his face on what remained of her robe making sure to rub against her bare breasts in the process.

Still sitting astride Jossy, grinding his pelvis into her, Neally snarled. "Now, this is the way it's going to be little lady. I'm going to have you and there's nothing you can do to stop that. Not one damn thing, you hear me? Might as well settle back and enjoy. I know I will. It can be good for both of us or just me. It's up to you."

Jossy stopped struggling beneath him. "You're a pig."

Neally slapped her hard enough to make her nose bleed.

"That's not nice little lady." He rose up, grabbing a handful of her coal black hair and using it, pulled Jossy to her feet. He practically dragged her into the bedroom throwing her on the bed. When she started to get up, he hit her hard in the solar plexus. Jossy gasped and fell back on the bed, incapacitated.

While Jossy was gulping air like a fish out of water, Neally pulled off his clothes until he was standing naked before her. She refused to look and kept her eyes closed tight. He ripped what remained of the robe off her.

Jossy, still gasping for breath, crossed her arms over her bare bosom and tried to turn away. Neally would have none of that. Never in his life had he seen such beauty. Those breasts were the most perfect ever he lay eyes upon. He forced her to stand then pushed her into the corner of the room, running his hands over Jossy's perfect body, grinding and probing until they both were breathing hard.

"The first time I saw you, I knew you wanted this, little lady. I have a sense of when women want me." Neally moaned and pressed his hard manhood against her.

"You disgust me." Jossy replied.

"Sure I do. You keep right on being disgusted." He rubbed a hard nipple with one hand and squeezed her ass cheek with the other.

Despite her true feelings on the matter, her body was responding to this assault. She felt betrayed on a level men never understand or can even imagine.

Neally picked her up and laid her naked body back on the bed forcing her legs wide open, entering her in one smooth thrust. Jossy gasped then started crying. It was all too much.

After only a handful of thrusts, Neally cried out as he ejaculated deep inside her. Jossy had excited him beyond anything he had experienced before. He collapsed on top of her breathing hard.

Jossy pushed at him. "Get off of me, you pig."

"Not yet. I want to enjoy this." Neally mumbled as his cock started to deflate, pulling itself from his victim.

Jossy pushed harder. "Get off me... NOW."

The instant they were no longer connected was like a newborn's umbilical cord being cut. Neally moaned and felt aloneness descend once again.

From over his shoulder, Jossy could see movement behind the young gunman. She pushed again and Neally started to rise.

Neally sensed something was wrong the instant he turned his attention away from the girl, but he was too late. With a sound like breaking eggs, the, butt of the sawed off shotgun knocked him off Jossy and out cold. The blow sent him sprawling on the bedroom floor, his head bleeding from a nasty gash above his right ear.

Jossy looked up at her rescuer and moaned in even deeper fear. It was the face she had seen on the road to Sycamore. Only now, in the weak lamp light, she had a much better look at it and it was even more horrible than she remembered. His face was melted and the eyes bottomless black pits. She cringed and scrambled to the farthest corner of the bed away from this apparition.

"Ma'am, you all right?" His gravely voice asked. The man went to the dresser and picked up the lantern moving it to the headboard. Now its light shown on the good side of his face.

"Oh god." Jossy sobbed and pulled a blanket over her

nakedness, watching him. When would this end? She has already been raped and now this monster is in her bedroom threatening her with more of the same or worse. She whispered. "Who are you?"

The man opened his duster revealing something shinny. Still holding the blanket with one hand, Jossy stared at it numbly.

"Deputy U.S. Marshal, you're a lawman?" Jossy said feeling a little hope grow within her.

"Yes ma'am."

Jossy looked again upon his face. Now, with the lantern throwing light mostly on the undamaged side, the guy didn't look like a monster at all. In fact, if you only looked at this side of his face, their was a kindness to him. And when you really looked at the bad side, it was pity and empathy she felt towards what had happened to him. He had been horribly burned yet he didn't let that stop him from being a marshal.

"Oh god, what took you so long?" The feeling of safety opened the emotional floodgates inside Jossy and she began to sob. Not little girl sobs like when they don't get their way. These were the gut wrenching sobs of a person at her wits end.

The marshal sat down on the bed and put his arm around Jossy. He held her until the worst was over. "Now, now. Don't waste no worry about him."

"Is he dead?" Jossy asked glancing at the inert form laying on her floor. Her ear was against the marshal's chest giving her a unique perspective on his unusual voice.

"Naw, not yet." The marshal responded. To Jossy, it sounded like a piece of heavy sandpaper rubbed powerfully across a school blackboard which through some miracle, produced syllables and words.

"What are you going to do with him?"

"You needn't worry 'bout that. Whatever it is, you can be sure he'll never bother you again. On that you have my word." The marshals voice was mesmerizing in its deep roughness and strange pronunciation, like he had his own special accent or perhaps his own mysterious language. She assumed it was due to damage he suffered when he was burned.

Jossy leaned back and looked up at him. "I'm Jossy Banyon and my husband is Ben Banyon. What's your name?"

"Deputy U.S. Marshal Levi Watt, ma'am. And I *was* here sooner, but had to wait till the man finished his business."

Jossy caught her breath. "What?" She pulled back.

The marshal stood and unlocked the back door. Turning back to her, he gazed lustfully down at the terrified woman. "Ma'am, you stay right there while I take care of this hombre. I'll only be a minute."

Utter fear gripped Jossy and she unwittingly whimpered. The marshal's obvious interest in her sent despair knifing through Jossy.

He took Neally by the wrist, dragging him out the back door. Jossy heard the body thump its way down the stairs. Scrambling from the bed, she watched them disappear out behind the privy. This marshal frightened Jossy more than Neally had.

"*Ahhhhhh!*" The strangely orgasmic sound came from the direction the marshal had gone. It sent a shiver down her spine, but Jossy didn't have time to dwell on it. She hurriedly put a dress on, but had no time for anything else. The thin cotton felt rough on her bare skin.

The marshal returned through the back door picking up Neally's clothes on his way to the fireplace in the main room. Taking up a poker, he added a couple pieces of wood to the smoldering coals and prodded it into a blazing fire. He added the clothes including the boots. The marshal stood there staring into the flame with a disturbed expression on his face.

She lit more lanterns and started a pot of coffee. "I've got coffee brewing." Jossy said from the kitchen end of the little house. She was more scared now then when she had been fighting Neally. Something about this man was telling her to run and another part was telling her if she did, getting caught would be fatal. The ease with which the marshal had dragged Neally's dead weight out of her house left little doubt of the man's strength. At under five feet tall and eight stones soaking wet, Jossy was just a slip of a girl compared to the marshal's bulk. He was almost three times her weight and bull strong.

"What did you do with him?" she asked.

The marshal scowled. "Thought I told you to not worry 'bout that?" He came over and rummaged through her cabinets. "Where you folks keep the liquor?"

She pointed. "Ah, my husband's brandy is in that cupboard right behind you." The marshal already had it in hand by the time she invited him to imbibe. "Help yourself."

The marshal squinted at the bottle's label. "What's this shit?" He uncorked and sniffed then took a long pull of the fiery liquid. "Bahh! Doesn't he have any real whiskey?" When Jossy shook her head. "Sodbuster." He took another long drink.

Jossy poured coffee and set the pot back on the stove. The frightened woman took her coffee cup in both hands and looked at the marshal over its rim. "What are you going to do?"

"You women, always asking questions." The bottle was quickly being emptied.

The marshal moved around the table until he was standing behind Jossy. She sat there without moving, the smell of fear rising from her like smoke from a forest fire. "A woman like you shouldn't be left alone."

"Ben, my husband, had to go to Prescott."

"Like I said, he shouldn't have left you alone."

"You're right, I should have spent the night with neighbors. I promise, that's where I'm going tomorrow right after chores. Mary invited me to stay with them until Ben gets back."

"Prescott, you say? Long way, Prescott."

"Yes. He's gone to buy seed, ours and the neighbors. We have over two hundred acres ready for planting." Jossy was babbling now. What else was she to do?

The marshal ran his finger over Jossy's bare neck, "Ain't right leaving a woman like you alone. Mighty tempting to a man. You sure you didn't encourage him some?"

"No, definitely not. I didn't do a thing. That bastard just broke in here. You shouldn't think for one minute I would cheat on my husband." Sliding out from under the marshal's attentions, she got up from the chair and moved across the kitchen away from him.

The marshal took another big swig of brandy. "That don't mean nothin. Just knowin' a woman's alone is enough for some. And you, bein' a special woman like you are, well, who can blame a man for doin' what the Good Lord intended. Go forth and multiply, isn't that what the good book says?"

"I don't think rape is what it means." Jossy was trembling now, openly frightened of the marshal.

The marshal let the last drop of brandy drip from the bottle to his tongue and slammed the empty down on the table with a bang. "Shit, out of whisky again. It's still hours before dawn. What do you think we should do?" His eyes locked on her chest and he grabbed his crotch. "Damn whore, can't you see what you're doin' to me? All I can think about is what you got under that dress. I know you ain't got no under garments on. I can see right through the way you're standing in front of the lantern."

Jossy moved away from the light.

The marshal shrugged. "Too late now. Little Frank is standing at attention and demands relief." He rubbed himself through his jeans as he moved around the table, the look on his face unmistakable. The devil had found a fresh soul to torment.

"No please, don't do this. You're a marshal. You're supposed to protect me." Jossy pleaded while keeping the table between them. At the proper point in this little dance, Jossy sprinted through the bedroom door and slammed it shut. She just managed to slide the bar in place before the marshal's big body tested the oak it was made of. Ben's homemade door lock held, at least for the moment.

Jossy ran to her armoire, grabbed her shoes and sprinted out the back door. She ran as fast as she could following the path to the outhouse and went by it in a flash. This was her land and she knew it like the back of her hand. The gully just past the privy would take her up to the plateau and it was only a mile to the Campbell's place. She already knew where she was going to stop and put on the shoes and had her escape route planned out.

She hadn't gone a hundred feet when she tripped over the body landing face first in a pool of blood. The blood had soaked into the ground some, but that only made it worse. Blood and mud covered Jossy from the top of her head down to her waist. She made some indecipherable sound and started to roll across the ground trying to get it off her, but only making it worse.

Getting hold of herself, she stopped and sat up. The body of Neally was lying face down on the trail, his feet higher than his head so his blood would drain. His face was turned to the side giving Jossy a clear view that his throat was slit ear to ear. The young woman started to cry. She never felt the noose coming until it was tightened around her neck. It was worse than useless to struggle.

"You're a mess. Now we need to get you cleaned up." The rope made it easy for the marshal to control Jossy. He made her stand then start back toward the house. "You can't get away from me. I hunt men for a living."

"Why are you doing this?" Jossy asked stumbling past the outhouse barefoot. She felt like a child under the control of an adult. The marshal towered over her and flung her about like she weighed nothing.

"No more questions." He tightened the noose until she choked then relented when he thought she got the idea. "From now on this is my party and you're my new toy." He gave the rope a tug to emphasize his meaning.

The man led her around the house to the horse trough by the barn. He picked her up and put her in. "Sit down." When she didn't move fast enough, he pulled the noose down. She fell to her knees in the water. The marshal then scrubbed the blood from her with one hand, keeping the noose taut with the other. He handled her more like a rag doll than a woman.

"There, all clean. Come inside and warm yourself." The marshal pulled Jossy to her feet where she stood in the trough, dripping wet. The thin cotton dress was now almost totally invisible. It clung to her body like wallpaper leaving little to the imagination. In the moonlight she looked like a goddess rising from her bath.

The marshal whistled softly. "You take my breath away Mrs. Banyon. You surely do. This is what I'm tellin' you. How do you expect a man to resist these charms? No real man could."

He pulled her out of the trough and towards the house. "You lead us on, just like you're leadin' me on right now. That's the way of you whores. Tease a feller till he can't take it no more."

Jossy looked up at the marshal, "Just leave, please leave."

"You want it as bad as I do, and I'm going to oblige you."

"Oh god…please just leave. I promise not to tell anybody about this." She begged him.

"This ain't nothin and don't you make somethin' out of this. It ain't no big deal. Means nothin' to nobody. If you was to go talkin' 'bout this to anyone, I'd come back here and finish what we started. You understand what I'm tellin' you." He pulled the noose tight around her throat.

"Yes." Jossy croaked.

"Good cause if that husband of yours ever comes lookin' for me, I'd have no choice, but to kill him." He led her through the house to the bedroom and slammed her down on the bed. "You don't want that, do you?" The thin cotton dress posed no real obstacle and was soon shredded. "Well, do you?" he brutally backhanded her across the face, splitting her lip.

"*Pig!*" she yelled and fought back with all the strength in her small body, flailing against the man's chest, pushing and pulling his shirt, ripping it. Ignoring her feeble efforts, he spread her legs with his knees and thrust himself inside her. As soon as he did, Jossy stopped all resistance and simply endured, her prize clutched in her hand. That did not mean the marshal stopped abusing her. He struck her again and again in rhythm with his thrusts, turning Jossy's face into a bloody pulp by the time he deposited his cum deep inside her, crying out as he did.

Exhausted, sweat pouring from him, his heart trying to pound its way out of his chest, he lay on top of her gasping for breath. She was the best he ever had. Better even than any of the whores he had known. He made up his mind right then, this would not be the last time he had Mrs. Banyon. She was too good to use just once.

He pushed Jossy off the bed and onto the floor where she landed with a thump. She lay there in a heap, naked and unconscious. He tied her up, hand and foot. The marshal didn't want any surprises during the night.

The man slept hard and fast. A gray dawn could be seen through the window when Lucretius jumped upon the bed awakening him. It didn't appear that Jossy had moved all night. The marshal knelt down beside her and checked for breath. Still breathing, but something was wrong. She was out cold and didn't seem to be in any hurry to wake up. He found several deep cuts on her head and she was bleeding from her ears. Damn, maybe he had been too rough with her last night. He untied her and put her in the bed dressing the worst of the wounds.

After running his hands all over her body, The marshal couldn't resist. He pulled her ass to the edge of the bed and raped her again. She never regained consciousness, never opened her eyes or moved a muscle. Not a single sound escaped her lips, but without the violence, the sex was unsatisfying. He pulled his pistol and would have shot her, but then he ran his hand over her perfect breast. No, not today. He would not kill this whore today. He left her there, naked and comatose, but alive.

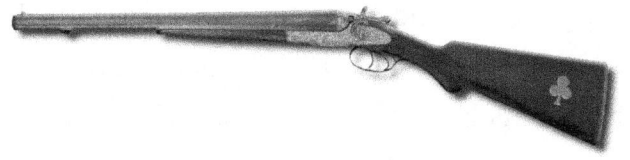

Ben Banyon

E verything dries out eventually. Descending into the Verde Valley from Jerome was a pleasant drive on a beautiful spring day in the Arizona Territory. Ben sat beside the mule skinner driving the freight wagon loaded with sacks of seed and admired his skill. Turned out that nine tons was the limit he could carry with one wagon. The old man kept his foot on the brake and never let his team of mules overexert themselves. Even so, Ben was relieved when they reached the bottom of Cleopatra Hill.

"Make the next left and my place will be just over the rise." Ben said to the driver.

"Got it. We'll have you unloaded before noon and I'll be on my way back to Prescott." The old man said giving the reins a little flip which did absolutely nothing as far as Ben could see. The mules plodded along at their own pace regardless of what the old skinner did.

"You're more than welcome to stay the night. Jossy would love to have the company." Ben said.

"Thank you kindly, but I should be getting back." The old

man had ideas about staying the night in Jerome. He had friends there and might even find some female companionship.

Turning that last corner, Ben leaned forward to catch the first glimpse of his holdings. To his surprise, his yard was filled with an extensive assemblage of wagons, many of them with their teams unhitched. Milling about in front of his house was a gathering of farmers and their families like he never seen before. The children were playing and even a couple of hounds were having a good time as they scuffled and ran about the yard.

One of the youngsters was first to notice the big freight wagon coming down the lane. *"He's here. He's here."* The little voice called out as the boy ran towards his elders.

The skinner rubbed his hand through his long beard nervously. "Seems you folks are needing this seed mighty bad."

"Pull up there in front of the barn." Ben looked among the crowd for Jossy, but couldn't find her. He did see Angus walking his way as the wagon was coming to a stop, but the look on the big Scotsman's face sent a chill down his spine.

Ben jumped off the wagon and started for the house still looking for Jossy. He didn't slow down as he went past Angus forcing him to reverse direction and hurry after him.

"Lad wait, I've something to tell you." Angus said matching pace with Ben.

Ben glanced at his friend, but didn't slow down. "So tell me."

A crowd had gathered at the bottom of the steps leading up to his front door forcing Ben to slow.

"Lad, there's been an accident."

This was enough to make Ben stop and give Angus his full attention. "Accident? What's happened? Tell me straight out. Is

Jossy hurt?"

"Aye, lad, she's been hurt."

Mary emerged from the house and crossed the porch looking down at the gathering. "Ya'll give him some space, let him through." When the crowd parted, Ben walked slowly through them and up the steps.

He wasn't aware that Angus was still at his side until he said. "Mary and me found her day before yesterday."

"Found her? Where?"

"There in the house, in her bed." Angus said.

Ben looked confused. "She had an accident in her bed?"

Mary finished what her husband couldn't. "She's been abused, Ben, terribly abused. Beaten to an inch of her life."

Ben was horrified. "That's no accident. Who did it?"

Mary shook her head. "Don't nobody know for sure."

Ben moved across the porch and entered his home, the home he had built with his own hands. Inside, he became aware that something had changed. It was the same table and chairs, the same old picture of President Lincoln on the wall, the same copy of the Farmers Almanac laying on the kitchen counter, but something was gone.

From pure habit, Ben hung his hat on the peg beside the door then went to the table and picked up the empty bottle of brandy. It had been almost full when he left.

Doc Morris came out of the bedroom, shutting the door behind him. "It's good to see you, Ben. Jossy is resting peaceful. I gave her something to make her sleep. She's been through quite an ordeal."

"What happened to her, Doc? Why won't anybody tell me?"

The man shook his head. "I'll tell you. She's been beaten within an inch of her life. By all rights, she should be dead, but she's not. She was unconscious when they found her and only woke up a few hours ago. I gotta tell you Ben, your wife is tough. I believe she will fully recover eventually, but you must give her time. Some wounds take longer."

"Sure, sure, Doc. Whatever you say. Can I see her?"

"Of course. She may still be awake, but I doubt it. I gave her enough bromide to put her out until at least tomorrow morning." Doc Morris said. He rubbed his jaw thoughtfully. "I know you two have not been married long. My best advice to you right now is to let your wife know how much you love her. Be patient, Ben. Jossy is in a very vulnerable state and needs every ounce of support you can muster." He came over to face Ben and looked into his eyes seeking even a smidgen of doubt. Doc Morris nodded in the affirmative. "Good. Make sure she knows how you feel. You can still lose her if you're not careful."

Ben stared back evenly. "I love my wife more than anything in this world. Whatever happens, that will never change."

"Good." Doc Morris said again with a grin. "Go to her, but if she's asleep, don't wake her."

Ben opened the door slowly, quietly, and entered the dimly lit room. The lantern was burning low over on their dresser and the armoire was standing open. He shut the door behind him without a sound and moved beside the bed looking down at Jossy.

She lay on her side facing him. Her right eye was completely swollen shut and both eyes were blackened from a broken nose. Numerous cuts and lacerations made the right side of her face, the side facing up to Ben, look like raw meat. Red and swollen, her lip had several deep cuts that had required stitches. Doc had left these open, but covered in a thick layer of salve to better heal.

Ben knelt beside the bed and brought his face up close to Jossy's and whispered. "My love, what have they done to you? I am so sorry."

To his surprise, Jossy opened her eyes and stared at Ben. Then she started to cry, not gut wrenching sobs, but big tears that slowly, one by one, welled up and escaped to roll off her face and soak the pillow. Then she abruptly pulled back and turned away muttering. "Don't look at me. You mustn't look at me."

Ben was stunned speechless for a moment. "Jossy, my love, this is all my fault. I should have never gone and left you alone. Who did this to you, Jossy?"

She pulled the blanket over her head and moved as far away from Ben as the bed allowed, right up against the wall. "Tell me, Jossy. I need to know." He reached out and touched her exposed arm which she jerked away.

"No... No... Go away... Leave me alone..." Jossy was now slurring her words and her voice trailed off.

Ben realized she had fallen asleep. He remained staring down at his wife. Nothing was worth this. He had failed her and that fact was driving a stake through his heart. Every heartbeat was like a bellows stoking a blacksmith's bed of coals to red hot. From this forge of vengeance, the hunter within him arose.

The expression that came over him was one of utter confidence. He knew exactly what he was going to do. He began here in his own bedroom to examine everything. There, on the floor, a blood stain and another there and there. The only real damage was to the lock on the bedroom door. It was completely smashed from the kitchen side.

Opening each drawer in the dresser, he didn't see anything amiss or out of place. Going to the armoire, he held up the lantern to see better and didn't find anything wrong until he tried to find her shoes. They were not here. He turned to the room and searched it quickly. Not many places for shoes to hide. No, they were gone.

Before leaving, Ben returned to stand over Jossy. He silently cursed the day he had the idea to form a seed co-op. Feeling utterly helpless, he had to do something, anything, or go crazy. "I promise you Jossy Banyon that whoever did this will pay." He said softly. Promises were easy. He reached out to take her hand. She had it clenched in a fist which he gently opened one finger at a time. To his utter astonishment, Jossy had something clutched so tight it was cutting into her palm. With some difficulty, Ben managed to remove it and took it to the lantern on the dresser where the light was better. It was an Deputy U.S. Marshal badge. There were several tiny flecks of what looked like dried blood on it. What would Jossy be doing with something like that? It went into his pocket.

He opened the back door examining it and the three stairs as he went down them finding smears of blood, but no damage. He followed the path towards the privy. People had trampled any prints that might have been there from the night of the attack, but Ben persisted.

Al Fortenberry was coming out of the privy as Ben came up the path and blurted out. "Going to go see where we found the body?"

Ben frowned. "Which body?"

"Ah, the body of that gunman, Neally. We found him just over the rise." He nodded his head in the general direction.

"Much obliged." Ben said moving past him. The path stopped at the outhouse, but he found several clear prints of a bare foot off the path and past the privy. He knelt and looked at each of them closely. "What were you doing out here Jossy, with no shoes on? Running for your life?"

He followed the track down the hill and soon came upon the dried blood. Ben was careful as he circled the area cataloging and analyzing every little detail.

"How many people have come here and looked at this?" Ben asked without looking up.

Angus had thought he had been quiet on his approach, but was obviously mistaken. "You look like an Indian, lad. You really know what you're looking at?"

"Answer me, who else has been here since you found Jossy?" Ben asked again.

Angus shrugged. "Myself, Tom, Lester and Doc Morris. That's it as far as I know."

"You forgot the dog."

"Oh, sure lad, it was Greyfriars that found him." The Campbell's dog was named for the most famous canine in all of Scotland, Greyfriars Bobby, a terrier who spent fourteen years guarding his master's grave.

"Found who?" Ben asked.

"Neally. You remember that young gunfighter who wanted to put a bullet in me?" Angus said.

Ben nodded, and pointed at something on the ground. "He

was there face down and from the amount of blood, his throat was slit. These marks are from his toes so he wasn't wearing boots and his head was downhill helping to drain the body. These are drag marks, but he wasn't dead yet, probably out cold. He was dead when Jossy ran from the house and tripped over him. This is where she put her hands trying to catch herself. Somebody wearing boots, the same boots that dragged Neally out here, came up behind her and they both headed back to the house."

"That's remarkable, lad. You can see all that in these little marks in the dirt?" Angus asked.

"Did you find Jossy's shoes?" Ben asked.

"That's downright spooky, lad. How did you know?"

"She's barefoot." Ben pointed to a clear footprint.

Angus frowned. "Oh... Then you should know that Neally was not only barefoot, but completely nude. Not a stitch of clothes on him."

The two men stood and stared at each other for a long moment, the unspoken question looming between them. It was Ben who spoke first. "She wouldn't cheat on me Angus. Not Jossy."

The tall man nodded not really believing it. "Sure lad. Jossy is a good wife."

"The second man did this. Maybe they were partners and one turned on the other. Or maybe he caught Neally in the act, killed him and then spooked Jossy?"

"Until Jossy starts talking, this is all just speculation. Come on, lad, let's go back to the house." Angus walked a few feet then stopped and turned back waiting on his friend.

Ben gave the scene one last sweep doing his best to memorize every detail, sighed and followed.

"Charles is getting the seed unloaded and divided up." Angus said.

Ben scowled. "I don't give a shit about seed, Angus. Right now, all I want to do is kill the bastard that hurt Jossy."

"It just might be Neally and he's already dead."

"I don't think so. I need to see the body. You haven't buried him yet, have you?"

"Ah, no. He's in the back of Doc Morris' buggy. They got a nice deep hole waiting for him at the cemetery." Angus replied.

"Good. I want to see it."

"Right now, lad?"

"Yes, right now." They came around the house and headed for the barn. The farmers were gathered outside, dividing the seed and loading it on their wagons. Many had already hitched their teams and were gone.

Ben went straight to the only buggy on the place. A blanket covered something in the back. He flipped it off revealing the young gunman lying on his back, his throat gaping open and his skin a sickly shade of pale. Ignoring the smell, Ben went over the body quickly, but thoroughly, stopping at the head wound and the cut in his shoulder. He paid special attention to the man's hands.

Angus watched him with interest. "What are you looking for now?"

"Look here, I'll bet it was Jossy that cut his shoulder, but this head wound knocked his ass into next week. I'm certain Jossy could never drag this guy from our bedroom to the woods. And look at his knuckles. Not a cut on them. This man did not put that beating on Jossy. No, that was the other man. I think you're right, the second man caught Neally in the act. What happened after that, we'll need Jossy to tell us."

Angus stood looking at Ben. "Who are you, lad? Where did you learn to do that?"

Before Ben could answer, Tom and his two sons pulled their wagon alongside Doc's buggy.

"Ben, we're all mighty sorry about what happened. Let us know if there's anything we can do for you or Jossy." Tom meant well, but insincerity practically oozed from his words.

Ben came over and accepted the man's hand. "Thanks Tom. As a matter of fact, there is. Could your missus work with some of the other ladies and stay with Jossy for a few days? I don't want her to be left alone again."

Tom looked apprehensive. "You're going after the person who did this? Why not let the law find them?"

"By the time the law gets here, the trail will be cold. This is my responsibility."

Trail? This is the first he heard of it. Angus cleared his throat. "Lad, Mary and I will be more than happy to stay with Jossy. Or we could move her to our place. Lord knows we have room for her. It would be no problem." Angus was hurt that Ben had not come to him first. Did he blame him for what had happened?

"I've already asked too much of you." Ben said to the big Scotsman.

"No, you haven't." Angus said then waved Tom on. "You go on Tom, I will take care of this and if I need help, I will let you know."

That was what Fortenberry wanted to hear. He had a ton of work ahead of him clearing fields and getting this seed in the ground. He felt for Ben and Jossy, but when he came right down to it, this wasn't his problem.

"Be sure you do. You be careful Ben. Vengeance is mine, sayeth the lord. You remember that." He gave his reins a good whip. "HYAAA!" It wasn't long berfore the yard was empty except for the Doc's buggy and Campbell's wagon.

"Lad, if you're going after this killer, I'm coming with you." Angus followed Ben into the barn.

Ben shook his head. "No, that just won't do. Someone needs to stay at home and make sure things get done that needs doing." He pointed to the six big bags of seed that was his and Campbell's then started saddling the black mustang as he talked. "I don't know how long I'll be gone, a week or two at best, but it might be longer. The fields are all plowed and won't wait. If you can get the planting done for me, I will forever be in your debt." Ben said.

Angus waved his hand. "Consider it done, lad."

The bag from the Prescott trip was next to the seed and had more than enough food inside. He transferred most of it to his saddlebags. Ben filled a canteen and stepped up on the black. He brought the horse close to the big Scotsman and leaned down. "If you can't do this for me, do it for Jossy?"

"Aye, lad, I can and will do it for both of you." The men shook hands. "I am truly sorry for what happened. I wouldn't blame you if you blamed me for it."

"Angus. Not at all. This was not your fault."

The thunder of hooves interrupted their parting. The black fidgeted beneath Ben hearing the approach of other horses. "Whoa boy, easy." He patted the horse's neck soothing him.

Angus moved to the barn door. "It's that rancher, Perkins and some of his men."

Ben frowned and stepped down, leading the black out of the barn. Emmett was at the front of six riders and a pack horse. They seen Ben and Angus and pulled up in front of them.

"Heard you was back." Emmett swung out of the saddle and stepped forward his hand extended.

Ben hesitated then shook his hand.

"I'm awful sorry Ben 'bout what happened. It's a real shame what's become of this land. Lawlessness and thievery at every turn." Emmett nodded to Angus who nodded in return.

"What can I do for you Mr. Perkins?" Ben asked.

Emmett looked the black over. "I see you're headed somewhere. Goin' after someone particular?"

"Might, but I don't see it's any your concern." What had started out as a great day had turned into a nightmare and he just wasn't feeling neighborly right then.

Emmett nodded taking none of it personal. "You must have some idea who done it otherwise this would just be running away and I don't see you as the running kind."

Ben visibly tightened up. "I got an idea."

"Then you wouldn't mind if me and my men went along?"

Ben scowled. "Yes, I mind. This is my fight."

Emmett nodded again, completely amiable. "Can't argue with that. No sir, not a bit, but you're wrong if you think its not my fight too."

Ben frowned. "How you figure that?"

"Because this is my country too. I'm rasing my family here, building a life here, and when my neighbor is wronged, then it's my duty to stand with him." Emmett said.

This from a rancher dead set against farmers homesteading the Verde Valley? Ben stood speechless for a moment then shook his head. "No sir. I don't want nobody coming with me. What I got to do, I do alone."

Emmett shrugged. "You're going to kill the bastard, I understand that. And I have no problem helping you do it. Now tell me who it is."

Angus looked at Ben and realized that his friend did know who it was. He had watched Ben track and conclude all sorts of things today and now this. "Who is it, lad?" He blurted out. "I can see it in your face, you know who it is."

Ben looked from one to the other and then up at the ring of cowboys sitting on their horses all looking down at him.

"Remind me to never play poker with you Angus." Ben growled. "I don't have a name, just this." Ben reached into his pocket and pulled out the Deputy U.S. Marshal's badge letting it lay face up in the palm of his hand so everybody could see it.

"That's a marshal's badge!" Hollister exclaimed from his horse. His next thought scared him so badly that he unconsciously backed his horse away from Ben.

Emmett reached for the badge and Ben let him take it. "No way to tell whose it is. It's just a piece of tin with some fancy engraving."

Hollister shook his head. "Only one marshal in these parts I know of and that's Kingsley. I ain't goin' against that son of a bitch. I heard what he did to them Almers and want no part of him. I'm sorry Mr. Perkins, you can fire me if you want, but I ain't goin'"

"Kingsley?" Emmett rubbed his chin in thought. "This will take some planning. You go off half cocked and you'll get yourself killed for sure."

"Taking a posse isn't a good idea. So many men will just warn him we're coming and get a lot of good men killed. I'm better alone. Then I don't worry about nobody, but me." Ben said.

Emmett hears confidence in the man's tone and sees it in his demeanor. It was more than simple bravado or anger over what happened to his wife. "You were in the war, wasn't you Ben."

Ben is taken aback. "So?"

"What did you do?"

"I don't talk about it." Ben snapped.

Emmett looked thoughtful. "You must have been what, *eighteen* during the war?"

The cowboy on the far right spoke up. "We all fought in the war. Lou, Hank and Joseph wore gray. The rest of us wore blue, but that was a time ago and we moved on. You won't get any blow back from us no matter which side you was on."

Emmett politely waited for his man to finish then said with a hint of sarcasm. "Thank you Roy for that moving testament." Tuning back to Ben. "But he's right. You will not be judged, at least by us."

"Iron Brigade." Ben said, then wished he hadn't.

The reaction among the cowboys surprised Angus. Those two words sat the men back in their saddles and their expressions changed.

"You was a Black Hat?" Hollister asked as if he didn't believe it.

Ben gave him a look that scared Hollister so bad, his own horse sensed it and skittered sideways into one of the other animals.

"Hollister, get that critter under control. Your horse can smell fear. " Emmett turned to Ben. "I agree, it'll be just the two of us. I'll go with you."

Hollister dismounted and calmed his horse over by the corral, far enough away to not be mistaken as a volunteer, but close enough to hear everything going on.

"I have no idea where to start looking so the trail may be long. It wouldn't be right taking you away from your ranch. That wouldn't be fair to you or your family." Ben said. "Don't worry about me, I can take care of myself."

"Glad to hear that. I'm counting on it, in fact. Hollister, get over here."

The cowboy shuffled over. "Yes sir?"

"Let me get this straight, Kingsley had a shoot out with the Almers and Red Jack got away, right?"

Hollister nodded. "Yes sir."

"Anybody else get away?"

Hollister nodded. "Yes sir. Some Indian breed named Clancy or Yancy or something like that."

"Do you think Kingsley will go after Red Jack or the Indian?"

Hollister frowned in concentration then nodded. "Definitely Red Jack. The way Otis told it, Kingsley seemed happy Red Jack got away."

"If Kingsley is still in these parts then so is Red Jack. All we got to do is find Red Jack before Kingsley does and then wait for him to show up." Emmett said.

Ben stared at the rancher thinking through what the man had said. It made sense. "How can you be sure he'll come after Red Jack?"

Emmett shrugged. "Nothing's ever a hundred percent. Which direction did he take out of Sycamore?"

"Ah... Kingsley or Red Jack?" Hollister asked.

"Red Jack." Emmett growled impatiently.

Hollister rubbed his stubble beard. "Ah, let's see... I think he would have gone north the way Quinn told the story. Yah, I'm sure of it. North. Quinn also thought Kingsley wounded Red Jack. In his leg."

Emmett shook his head. "He wouldn't have gone north. North is what he wanted Kingsley to believe which might be why Kingsley come upon Ben's place."

"Sure, makes sense that he would have turned west into the Black Hills." Ben was beginning to appreciate Emmett and how his mind worked. "I've seen the smallest wound kill a man in a few days. There's a doctor in Jerome or all the way in Prescott if he needs one and if that's not possible, someplace to rest up until he can travel." Ben said.

"I know every old cabin, cave and trail along that range. We'll go check them out, one by one on our way to Jerome. We'll find him." Emmett said.

Ben finally nodded. "I still don't know why you want to risk your life helping me, but I'll take it. I accept your offer to come along and hope you never regret it."

Emmett laughed. "So do I, Ben. So do I. Let's ride. Our first camp is three hours away."

Watching them ride away trailing the packhorse behind,

Angus asked. "What's a Black Hat?"

Hollister rubbed his stubble again. "Being a foreigner like you are, why would you know any American history?"

"I am not a foreigner, Hollister, but I am ignorant of many things. Enlighten me."

Hollister looked at him strangely. He didn't know what the word meant, but it sounded like he wanted him to light him on fire? Naw, that can't be it. "Black Hats was the troops that lead the Union into battle at Brawner's Farm, Bull Run, South Mountain, and Antietam. Ever hear of Stonewall Jackson? The Iron Brigade was the only ones to defeat him. Yes sir. The Black Hats were first in battle and last to leave, that is if they lived."

"I learn something new about my friend every day. He has never mentioned the war at all." Angus said.

"Don't take it personal. After a man goes through somethin' like that, they generally don't want to talk about it, especially to friends and family. Don't want them thinking you're some kind of animal. Now if you'll excuse me, I've work waitin'." He stepped up on his horse and followed the other cowboys back towards the Pitchfort Ranch, thankful that Mr. Perkins hadn't insisted he go with them chasing after that Marshal Kingsley. Only then did it occur to him that he may never see Mr. Perkins ever again. Damn, and he just got this job.

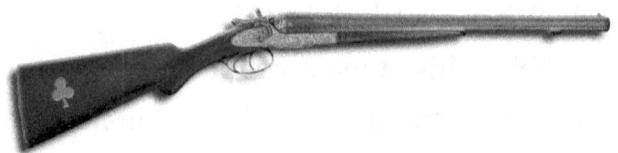

Morning came and after a quick breakfast, Ben took the horses down to the Verde to let them drink their fill. Leading them back to the camp, Ben saddled both horses while Emmett tied the gear to the packhorse. "There's a cabin just over that hill about a mile. Good place to start."

Ben swung into the saddle. "You think he might be holed up there?"

"Maybe, but we act like he is. We'll go in on foot the last few hundred yards and you creep in to scout if it's occupied. I'll move in close and cover you as best I can, but understand, I'm not as young as I used to be." Emmett shook his head like an old bear.

"You bring that fancy new rifle?" Ben asked

"Sure and a few hundred rounds to go with it. These are special rounds, over packed with gunpowder. They increase the range by a hundred yards at least."

"That's a thing about us humans, we're always looking for new ways to kill each other." Ben didn't laugh.

"You'll be glad I have it before this trip's done." Emmett said.

"No doubt." Ben replied.

The cabin was empty and the next and the next. The day blurred into one long series of maneuvers that exhausted Ben by mid afternoon.

Emmett pulled his horse alongside Ben's. "The Lakota Sioux

have a story about the rabbits. Seems that all the rabbits had become very depressed and felt worthless. Why? They had been told by their leaders to run back to their burrows whenever a stranger appeared and not come out until they had passed."

"The rabbits all did what they were told so well that even the chirp of a little cricket would send them scampering to their dens. But run-and-hide cowardice will eat at a rabbit just like it does a man and eventually the rabbits had all become seriously ill." Emmett grinned devilishly.

"Then one day the rabbits held a great council, and after talking over everything for a long while with no end in sight, they finally left it to their medicine man to decide what to do. The rabbit medicine man arose and said: *My friends, it is clear we are of no use. There isn't a creature on earth that fears us, and we are so timid that we cannot defend ourselves, so the best thing for us to do is to rid the earth of our cowardice by all going over to the big lake and drowning ourselves.*" Emmett said.

"So off to the lake they went and were about to jump in when they heard a whole passel of splashing along the waters edge. Seems when they came to the shoreline, it scared the frogs into jumping into the lake." Emmett said.

"The rabbit medicine man stopped everyone. Here clearly was a creature afraid of rabbits Now they no longer felt so cowardly. They went home, fat and happy." Emmett said.

"That's quite a story. What's the point?" Ben drank from his canteen.

Emmett sighed. "Isn't it clear? Had it not been for frogs we would have no rabbits. I've seen it myself. Watch the rabbits coming to the edge of a lake and the frogs just go nuts."

Ben looked sceptical. "You seen it yourself?"

"It's getting late and by the looks of that sky, we can expect rain tonight." Emmett recognized the signs in Ben. The man was a fine physical specimen, but what he was doing would wear out the strongest among us. "There's an old cedar pole shack up this canyon. My boys have been known to use it to get out of weather on occasion. We make it and we'll sleep dry tonight. What do you say? You got one more scout in you?"

"Lead out. I'll follow." The trail here allowed them to ride side by side which they did, setting a leisurely pace. The horses were just as tired as the men.

"It's going to be dark by the time we get there so take special care." Emmett warned.

Ben yawned. "Right, special care."

"That's what I thought. I'll take this one Ben. You hang back and cover me."

"The hell you say. We ain't switching it up at this late date. I'll scout, you cover."

"Does anyone ever win an argument with you Ben? 'Cause is seems like you never compromise." Emmett didn't sound pleased. He was used to people doing what he commanded.

"Not when it may cost someone their life, I never compromise."

"So you're saying I can't do your job?" Emmett was just messing with him, but these things are always half serious.

Ben remained quiet because that's exactly what he thought.

Emmett scowled. "I'll have you know, I fought in the war too. I might be older than you, but I can still get it done."

Ben realized he had opened a door. "Where'd you fight?"

"What? Ah, I don't want to talk about it."

"I know the feeling." Ben said sarcastically.

They road in silence for a spell then Emmett finally said. "I was captured at Gettysburg in '63 and spent the rest of the war in Elmira Prison. Not a fun place to be, let me tell you."

Ben could hear the pain in the older man. "Mr. Perkins, if you don't want to talk about it..."

"The war tore my family apart. My brother was Yankee and I was Rebel. My son fought and died at Gettysburg. He thought slavery was wrong, but fought on the side of the Confederacy anyway."

"Why did he do that?" Ben asked.

"Honor? Loyalty? Habit? I don't really understand it myself."

Ben had also fought at Gettysburg, but he couldn't find it in him to say it. It would be too much like him telling this man he had put him in prison and killed his son. Death had walked beside Ben that day and reaped a bountiful harvest. It was something he tried to forget without much success. Images still haunted him and he feared they would never go away.

Thunder rolled across the sky putting an end to the conversation. The approaching storm was getting closer by the minute.

"Better find some shelter fast or we're going to get wet." Emmett said.

"Might do you some good, Mr. Perkins. I know I'd appreciate it." Ben deadpanned.

"Ben, is that a joke? I think that's the first breath of humor you've shown since we set out."

Lightning struck a snag of a tree on the other side of the canyon and the horses bolted sideways. Even though they were bone tired, both men kept their seat. When the horses were under control again, Emmett pulled up and they dismounted.

"The cabin is just past those rocks. I'll stay with the horses so they won't spook in this weather." Emmett had a firm grip on the reins of the three horses, but he knew that would not be enough if they decided to run. "Think I'll put the hobbles on them just to be safe."

Ben nodded. "I'll help." Lightning flashed and lit up the forest. The black didn't like lightning and liked hobbles even less. It took Ben several minutes of convincing before he was ready to go. "Be back soon." He disappeared into the trees.

Keeping night vision is difficult in a lightning storm. After every flash he had to stop and wait while his eyes readjusted, but it wasn't long before he found what he was looking for. The cabin was a dark mass at the edge of a clearing close to the bottom of the canyon. Ben kept to the bushes and circled. He was almost ready to go in when he heard something in the wind.

The snort was not from one of their horses. They were all down the canyon and well out of earshot. He waited for the next lightning flash. There, in the trees a few yards from the cabin's door, the unmistakable outline of a horse.

Ben crept around until he was able to find the saddle in the bushes. The horse seen him and whinnied. Ben spoke softly and run his hand along its flank calming the animal.

He headed back to get Emmett. The rain started coming down hard long before he got there. Lightning was now almost a constant shimmer above him and thunder rocked the hills every so often. It was working itself up to a big blow. The little creek in the bottom of the canyon might not stay little if it rained like this much longer.

When Ben reached the horses Emmett was nowhere to be found. "Wish you could talk." Ben stood close to his black, draping his arm around the big neck, talking in his ear and looked around. Rain came in sheets beating on the forest. The wind raced down the canyon whipping everything in sight into a frenzy. Lightning flashed sending shadows scurrying hither and yon. Nothing was at rest. The forest was alive with movement.

"Red Jack's inside the cabin." Emmett said from the other side of the black.

Ben jumped at the first sound. "*Shit*. God damn it Mr. Perkins. That's a good way to get shot."

"No light and no fire as far as I can tell. He may be dead." Emmett pointedly ignored his younger companion's scare.

Ben shook his head and glared at Emmett from under the brim of his hat, the flickering lightning making him look devilish. "Fine, you can still get the job done, but don't ever do that again."

Emmett smiled. "Red Jack's not going anywhere. Let's wait for the worst of the storm to pass and he's asleep before we go in after him. No need getting shot by this hombre."

Ben scowled and untied the poncho from behind his saddle. "I'll be in those rocks where I can see the cabin."

"I never feared you would shoot me, Ben. You're much too good for that. And drop the mister. Call me Emmett. If we're riding together then it's only right."

Ben stopped. "I was at Gettysburg." He blurted out. "I just thought you should know. If you don't want to go in with me, now's the time to leave. I wouldn't hold it against you. You have already helped far beyond what a body could expect and I thank you."

"Leave? Just when the fun starts?" Emmett retrieved his own poncho and a lantern from the packhorse. Lightning flashed and a particularly large thunder boomer rocked their world. "And Ben, Gettysburg is part of our past, but not part of our future unless we make it so which I have no intention of doing. Wounds never heal if we are constantly picking at the scab. I hold no animosity towards you."

Ben stood silent and waited until Emmett was beside him. "I'm not proud of what I done during the war, but I also don't want to live my life making amends for those things."

"Then don't." Emmett put his hand on Ben's shoulder. "Come on, Ben. Let's find a nice dry rock to sit on."

Ben smiled for the first time in days. "Good luck with that."

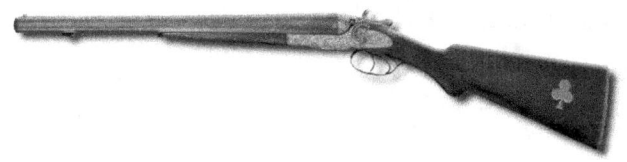

Red Jack Almer

It was pitch black inside and out. The rain had stopped and the lightning was down to just a weak flicker now and then. Clouds still blocked the moon and stars.

Ben entered the cabin first, opening the door only far enough to squeeze through then quickly shutting it behind him. He didn't want to get silhouetted by a flash of lightning. Ben stood motionless, listening and letting his eyes adjust as much as they would.

He could hear ragged breathing from somewhere at his feet. With his pistol in one hand, he used his other thumbnail to spark a match. In the sudden flare, he could see the man lying on his side in front of an old potbellied stove, his back to him.

Ben quickly disarmed him and called out. "Come on in. I don't think this bastard is going to be shooting anybody today."

The door opened letting in a gust that blew out Ben's match.

Ben stepped further into the room making sure if Red Jack suddenly started shooting, that he wasn't where he was a second before. He lit another match. Red Jack hadn't moved.

Emmett struck his own match and lit the lantern. Examining

the man, he quickly determined that Red Jack was out cold. Ben touched his forehead. "Running a fever. He's burning up."

"Don't surprise me none. Bullets are nasty little devils. Check to make sure he ain't got a knife or a holdout gun somewhere." Emmett hung the lantern from a nail then knelt beside Red Jack and turned him on his back. "He's lost a lot of blood."

The man moaned and thrashed about weakly, but didn't regain consciousness.

Emmett pulled the blade he kept in his boot and cut Red Jack's pant leg open from the knee to the belt line and frowned. "Lucky we found him when we did. Another day or so and this would be gangrenous. As it is, we got to get that bullet out."

"I'm no doc. You going to do it?" Ben asked.

"Well, there's only the two of us and if you're not going to do it, that leaves me. Don't look so relieved, you're going to help. First thing is get the horses up here and bring in my black bag. You'll find it in the west side of the pack under the foodstuff. Oh, and the rope, bring the rope."

Ben made one more quick search of the cabin around Red Jack and Red Jack himself. He thought the man was out, but he wasn't one to assume anything.

By the time he got back, Emmett had a fire going in the potbellied stove and water heating in a beat up tin basin. Ben had the little black bag and the rope slung over his shoulder. "You a doc? For real?"

"That's a doctor's bag, true, but I haven't practiced medicine since the war. Other than on my own critters. I'm a pretty good vet if I do say so myself."

"You pull out many bullets from your critters?" Ben asked.

Emmett chuckled. "No, can't say as I have, but I did while I was in Elmira. I don't think I've forgotten how it's done."

"Oh... What you want me to do?" Ben asked.

"You're going to hold him down while I go in and get the bullet. It looks like it missed the bone, but it didn't go through so it's in deep. Red Jack ain't gonna like this much. Wish we had a couple more men to hold him, but we don't. First thing, let's tie his arms and legs so he can't hit back. Then we make his life miserable. From what I know about Red Jack Almer, that part may be fitting. He deserves whatever we do to him."

Emmett opened the little iron door on the stove and sterilized his probe and tongs in the fire. "Sit on his chest and get ready to fight." He put his full weight on Red Jack's lower legs which were lashed together. "Here we go." He began to push a long straight probe into the wound.

Red Jack screamed and thrashed about. Ben put all his weight on the man and wished he had gagged him as well. He'd never heard a man make such a noise.

Once he started, Emmett worked at a steady pace and never let up. Ben thought it strange that Emmett didn't watch what he was doing, but stared off into space as he twisted and turned that piece of metal in Red Jacks leg.

"There!" Emmett exclaimed triumphantly. "I found it." He took the long slender tongs designed for this very thing and slid them into Red Jack alongside the probe. A moment later. "Got it." He pulled the tongs, the probe and the bullet out with one smooth motion punctuated by Red Jacks heart rending scream, then all was quiet.

Ben got off the now still man and looked closely at him.

"He's still breathing, but out cold."

"To be expected. It's a body's way of dealing with things when they get too rough."

"What now?" Ben asked.

"Dress the wound and wait. Either Red Jack will wake up in a few hours or he won't."

Ben nodded. "I'll go get us some firewood and bring in the rest of the gear."

Emmett nodded. "Good job."

Ben shrugged. "All I did was hold him down. You did the heavy lifting. Pretty slick Doc. Nary a wasted motion. Went right in and took it out."

"Don't call me doc. Never call me that." Emmett replied with an edge.

"Sure Emmett. Forget I said it." Ben didn't know what nerve he had touched, but was more than willing to abide his wishes.

The Arizona sun had burned off the clouds during the day, but it was now sinking behind the Black Hills leaving a chill in the air. Down in the canyon, sunset came early, but took its time finishing up. Dusk was a drawn out affair that wasn't in any big hurry.

The little creek had run full throughout most of the day, but was finally returning to its normal trickle. The ground within the canyon was still damp, but it too was drying out quickly. Storms didn't stick around for long here.

Emmett sipped hot coffee. "Even if he don't wake up, we need to get him to a doctor. Camp Verde is closest. We'll start first thing tomorrow."

"I ain't goin' to Camp Verde." Red Jack mumbled and opened

his eyes.

"Welcome back." Emmett came over to look down at him. "Glad you're awake."

"Who're you?" Red Jack mumbled.

Emmett picked up the canteen and held it to Red Jack's lips. "Slowly. Don't drink so fast."

Red Jack slurped and gulped until Emmett pulled it away.

"My name is Emmett Perkins and this is Ben Banyon. I own the Pitchfork Ranch and Ben has a homestead on the Verde. Lucky we found you or you'd be dead. I doubt if you would have ever regained consciousness."

"Yah? Well... Thanks." Red Jack wasn't sure what was going on, but he was naturally suspicious.

"What's your name?" Emmett asked. "You had no papers on you so you're a mystery."

"Oh..." Red Jack hesitated as he thought about things.

Emmett kept the smile from his face watching Red Jack process this information and come up with a lie.

Red Jack hemmed and hawed. "Well, ah... Sam. Sam Teller. From Saint Louis." He held his hand out.

Emmett did smile then, a broad cheerful expression that disarmed Red Jack completely. He shook his hand. "Sam Teller from Saint Louis, very glad to make your acquaintance. What are you doing out here?"

"Ah, well, ah, I was on my way to California when someone shot me. If you hadn't come along, I don't know what I'd a done."

Emmett smiled even broader. "You would have died Sam. You was half way there when we found you."

"OK, I did thank you didn't I?"

"Certainly. And you're welcome. Now tell us why you can't go to Camp Verde. That is where you'll find the nearest doctor."

"Ah, well, ah, the guy who shot me might still be there."

"Who might that be?"

"Ah, well, I can't say for sure. The guy had a scarred face."

"I see." Emmett said. "Where would you like us to take you?"

"Ah, well, maybe I could just go on to California like nothing happened. I don't carry no ill will to the man."

"That's very kind of you Sam. I'll tell you what, you come with us to Camp Verde and see the doctor there, then you can be on your way."

"Camp Verde?" Red Jack slurred. He was bone tired. He had never felt this exhausted before. He couldn't keep his eyes open or his mind in gear. "Sleep... I need sleep. Talk later." He closed his eyes and drifted away.

"Sure Sam, get some sleep." Emmett smiled at Ben and held his finger to his lips signaling quiet. Then he motioned to go outside. The two men went to where the horses were staked out. Ben rubbed the black behind his ears.

"We'll start tomorrow morning. Red Jack should be fit to ride by then and if he ain't, we tie him to the saddle." Ben was done with waiting.

Emmett nodded. "Agreed. He's ready to travel."

"I'll get us packed." Ben said.

The next morning Red Jack woke up to the smell of coffee and beans. "God, I'm hungry. Can I have some of those?"

Emmett plopped a generous portion into a tin plate and brought it over to Red Jack. "Here, let's get you sitting up."

"Much obliged." Red Jack winced, but sat up and took the tin from Emmett. He scooped the warm beans into his mouth not caring when a few didn't make it.

Ben came in from outside and picked up some more of the gear. "I see he's woke up."

Red Jack looked from one to the other and continued to eat. "Where's my pistol and rifle. I don't feel right without them."

"Sorry Sam. They wasn't here when we found you. You sure you had them?" Emmett replied.

"Huh? What you mean, they weren't here? Where else would they be?" Red Jack frowned.

"Just what he said, your holster was empty and no rifle to be found. No food either or a bedroll. There was just you laying on the floor like you was dumped there or something." Ben said. "Strange for a fellow on his way to California."

"Ah, maybe someone took them and my gear?" Red Jack said.

"That's what we figured, Sam. Someone got here before us and took your stuff." Emmett said. "Funny, they left your clothes and an extra pair of boots. Here, try them on." He held out a pair of boots to him.

Red Jack took them and stared for a moment then threw them to the floor. "No! Them's Tom' boots. Where'd you get them?"

"Who's Tom?" When Red Jack stayed quiet, Ben shrugged. "They was right over there. What's the matter? You look like you seen a ghost or something."

"Damn oh damn, yes, let's get outa here." Red Jack said.

Emmett and Ben looked at each other and they both worked it out about the same time. If those were Tom Almer's boots then

Kingsley had been here. If Kingsley knew about this cabin then they were all in danger. It was time to move.

Ben picked up the last of the gear and went to the door opening it a bit to peer outside. He stayed there for several long moments before going on out and then, he scanned the surrounding forest carefully as he worked.

He led the saddled horses and the pack horse over to the cabin. Emmett emerged with Red Jack leaning heavily on him and complaining about how much it hurt. He helped him get on the horse.

Stepping up on the black, Ben led them out trailing the pack horse. Emmett followed leading Red Jack's horse.

"I can ride myself. Don't need you to lead my animal." Red Jack said.

Emmett shook his head. "You're hurt and might fall off. Can't risk it."

"Bull shit. Give me my reins." Red Jack replied.

Ben picked up the pace. Emmett ignored Red Jack and did the same. Red Jack soon was in too much pain to care who was leading or who was following. It was all he could do to keep his seat.

Emmett directed Ben to take a different route from the canyon back towards Sycamore. They soon found themselves riding along the banks of the Verde River. It was swollen from the recent rain, but they made good time.

"How about stopping? I gotta make water and I could use something to eat." Red Jack said. They had been in the saddle for hours and his leg was killing him. He knew Sycamore was just up ahead, but still didn't suspect anything. He planned to give these two the slip right now before they reached it.

Ben pulled up under a big cottonwood tree on the bank of the river. He stepped down letting the black and the pack horse wade in a few feet. He tied them to a tree branch at the edge of the river then looked up at Emmett. "What you think, about fourteen miles to Sycamore?"

He nodded. "Close enough."

Red Jack was suddenly wary. "I thought we was going to Camp Verde?"

Emmett sat his horse and held the reins of Red Jack's. "Naw, you know this is the way to Sycamore, Red Jack. You been there before. Remember? You had a gunfight with Marshal Kingsley. That's who put that bullet in your leg."

Red Jack gripped the saddle horn and glared first at Emmett then at Ben who came over and tied his hands together. "Damn! Not so tight." The outlaw shook his head realizing just how completely he had been fooled. "You lyin' sons a bitches."

"Whoa, listen to that, Ben. He says his name is Sam from Saint Louis on his way to California and we're the liars? I don't know where you got your schoolin', but the definition of lying is *not* telling the truth."

Being called a liar didn't even faze Red Jack. He couldn't care less. "You work for Kingsley? That son a of bitch wants to kill me. You takin' me to Kingsley?"

"Naw, nothin like that. You like to fish, Red Jack?" Emmett asked.

"What? You crazy? What's fishin' got to do with this?" Red Jack asked.

"Well, I'll tell you. When you go after that big catfish hiding deep in the pond you need the right bait. You're our bait. We're countin' on Kingsley coming after you."

Red Jack sat on his horse letting this sink in. "***You two are crazy!*** Kingsley's gonna eat you for supper. A rancher and a farmer gonna take on Kingsley? Holy shit. You ***must*** be crazy. No sir, I want no part of this. If you want to commit suicide, you don't need to take me along for company."

Ben pulled Red Jack from the horse making him cry out. "***Hey, watch it!*** Was that fun for you because it was a church social for me." Gripping the horn tightly, he leaned heavily on his horse or would have fallen.

"Shut up and piss or get back on the horse. Which is it?"

Red Jack unbuttoned and started to piss. "You know Kingsley murdered my wife? And my two brothers?"

Emmett nodded. "Tell your side and maybe we could help you?"

"I knew it. You two are ***not*** a couple a sodbusters! You're the law, ain't you?" Red Jack blurted.

Red Jack wasn't small, but below Ben's height and weight. Ben reached down and gripped Red Jack around the neck with one hand and drew his gun with the other pressing its muzzle against the outlaws head. The sound of the hammer cocking back was sharp against the burble of the Verde.

Red Jack's eyes grew wide and his breathing increased. He still had a hold of his cock and quickly put it away even as Ben stretched his neck.

"Take it easy big fella." Red Jack gurgled.

"I'm not a lawman. I'm the husband of a wife brutalized by Kingsley. I'm not going to arrest Kingsley, I'm going to kill him. You don't want to be standing in my way and right now that's what I see. You're in my way." Ben hissed in his ear

"I still say he should be alive to make good bait." Emmett said from the back of his horse. He was leaning forward resting his elbow on his saddle calmly watching.

"And I say it don't matter. What say you *Sam*, what do you think? Is your breathing or not breathing going to make a smidgin of difference? I mean, Kingsley won't know you're already dead. Who's going to tell him?" Ben's breath was hot on Red Jack's check and his voice hypnotic.

"Ah, I will." Red Jack was sweating bullets and not thinking clearly. His normal reaction to pressure was a quick draw or a quicker retreat and neither was possible here.

Emmett laughed easing the tension just a bit. "Red Jack, that's the point. You'll be dead." Even Ben looked amused when he pointed the muzzle skyward and eased the hammer back down.

Red Jack was immensely relieved. "Good point. What do you want from me?"

"It's simple Red Jack. We want you to tell the truth." Emmett said.

"What?" Red Jack was shocked. "The truth?"

Emmett smiled. "I know that's a foreign language, but Ben and I will be there to spur you on when you falter."

Ben tapped Red Jack on the head with the barrel of his pistol.

Red Jack scowled. "The truth is hard to come by sometimes. Maybe you don't want to hear the truth?"

Ben brought the muzzle back down and cocked the hammer back. Red Jack cringed and would have shied away, but for the death grip Ben had on his neck. Instead, he whimpered and said.

"OK, OK, what do you want to know?"

"We want everything you know about Kingsley, especially these last few weeks. You said he murdered your wife and brothers? We want to know everything about that." Emmett replied.

"That might take awhile." Red Jack whined.

Ben released his hammer again and slid his pistol back in its holster. "You can tell us all about it as we ride and don't leave out anything. Now let's get you on that horse."

Ben practically picked Red Jack up and set him in his saddle. "Easy does it big fella." Red Jack got his boots in the stirrups and said. "What, no food? If you insist on killing me then at least don't starve me to death."

"You ate the last of our beans this morning. No food until Sycamore." Ben tied Red Jack's bound hands to the saddle horn and slipped a noose around the man's neck.

"Whoa! You don't need that." Red Jack said.

"Shut up." Ben growled. Pulling the noose taut, he handed the other end of the rope to Emmett who never left his saddle or his grip on Red Jack's reins. He wrapped the rope around his saddle horn making sure Red Jack watched.

"Let's go." Ben stepped up on the black and started off.

Red Jack yelped when Emmett took off after him. "Hold on, damn it! You're chokin' me." With his hands tied to the saddle horn and his neck in a noose, when his horse didn't keep up, the rope became tight.

"Keep talking and don't slow us down or you will finish this ride draped over the saddle, not sitting in it." Emmett was not the nice old man Red Jack thought he was.

Red Jack kicked his horse in the flank using his good leg. "Giddyup you flea bag, giddyup."

"Talk." Ben said.

"First I knowed that Kingsley was on my trail was finding Maggie gut shot in our cabin..." The miles rolled beneath the horse's hooves as Red Jack told them his story.

"So who shot the kid?" Emmett asked at one point.

"Don't know." Red Jack replied.

"Who was he?" Ben asked

"Don't know that either. Never seen him before." Red Jack said again. "That breed, Yancy, he said Kingsley shot the kid then Tom and I believed him. Look, I don't see as how this is helping you at all."

Emmett got them moving again and said. "Tell me more about this breed."

Red Jack took one look at Ben and kept talking.

The telegraph office was closed when the three men rode into Sycamore, but Emmett knew the operator and where he lived. He soon had him busy tapping away.

The first telegraph was to the territorial governor in Prescott informing them that Red Jack Almer was under lock and key here in Sycamore and they should send someone to pick him up. The second and third were to Camp Verde and Jerome letting the law there know where Red Jack was. They all told the story of Maggie's murder, Tom's hanging, and Marshal Kingsley's gunfight with the Almer Gang.

Emmett walked out of the office and looked up at Ben still sitting on the back of his horse. The other end of the noose around Red Jack's neck was wrapped tightly around his saddle horn. "It's been a long day. Can I buy you a meal, Ben?"

Red Jack brightened up. "Now you're talkin' Let's find a saloon and wet our whistle while were at it. I could use a whisky then thick steak and homemade bread with honey. Shit, I'm so hungry. I could eat an old shoe."

"A shoe is what you're going to find at the Tumbleweed. Otis doesn't cook." Emmett said.

"Stockman's cafe is still open. There's light coming from the windows." Ben said. He was hungry too.

"Lead the way." Emmett said.

Ben started walking his horse while leading Red Jack's. Emmett untied his horse and followed them a few feet behind.

"Can we take this rope off me? It's gonna be hard to eat with this 'round my neck." Red Jack said.

Tieing up outside the cafe, the rancher and the farmer loosened the noose and slipped it off. "It goes right back on when I say and no back talk. Got it?" Emmett said.

"Got it." Red Jack would have said anything to get it off. He rubbed his neck where the rope had chaffed it raw. "Who's gonna help me?"

Ben slide his arm around the man and let him lean heavily on him.

"Keep your weight off it and it should heal in a few days." Emmett said estimating the level of pain the man felt on moving it around.

There wasn't anyone else inside the little cafe at this late hour. Emmett nodded his greeting to the proprietor, the gray bearded man who took their order.

"Steak and eggs, Jeffrey, and coffee." Ben said.

"I was sure sorry to hear about what happened to your wife, Ben. Terrible thing." Jeffrey said.

"Thanks. What else have you heard? Anything recent?"

"The womenfolk put together a basket and took it out just today. I put up a pot of stew and a flat of corn bread and the mercantile supplied bread, some cheese, some beans. They're doing all right. The way I heard it, Jossy was mighty angry at you for going after the man who done it. Who done it anyway? Do you know?"

Ben laid his hat in a vacant chair. "That's mighty nice of all you folks to look after her and all. I don't know how I'll ever repay your kindness. Emmett? What are you having?"

"I'll have what you're having and the same for him." Emmett cocked a thumb at Red Jack.

Jeffrey stood silent for a moment until he realized there was no answer forthcoming. "Very good, Mr. Perkins. I'll have those steaks right out."

After the man had left, Red Jack chuckled. "You know you can't tell 'em what's coming. Kingsley's going to destroy this town and you in it. What you think they would say to that?"

Emmett laid the noose on the table. "Shut up, Red Jack."

"Fine, but you know what I'm sayin'. This." Red Jack tapped the table with his finger. "is not right. Somebody's gonna get killed. Me being back here's not a good idea."

After dinner, Emmett took them to a barn he used when he was in town. The tack room in the rear didn't have a window and the door was solid. They tied Red Jack's hands and feet then wedged the door tight shut at the floor. Ben stretched out in the nearest stall and was asleep in moments. Emmett looked down at him and smiled. He liked this young man.

Emmett took his saddle and set it outside the tack room door, laid down using it as a pillow and promptly went to sleep. That's where Hollister found them the next morning.

"Mr. Perkins, wake up, Mr. Perkins." Hollister was insistent, but careful not to get close enough to get kicked or shot.

Lying there with his eyes still closed, Emmett asked. "What is it Hollister?"

"Marshal Kingsley's in town." Hollister said.

Emmett opened his eyes and sat up. "When?" He stood and noticed Ben standing behind Hollister.

"'Bout an hour ago, I reckon." Hollister said.

"Why did you wait to tell us." Ben said making Hollister jump at the first utterance. He had not heard him come up behind him

"*Shit!* I didn't see you there, Ben." Hollister exclaimed then mumbled something about he shouldn't sneak up on a body.

"Where is he?" Emmett asked checking his pistol.

"Sittin' on the front stoop of the Tumbleweed Saloon, bold as brass. He's daring you to come after him."

Ben turned to go and Emmett reached out to grasp his arm. "That's what he wants, Ben. Don't fall for it. You take him head on and he has every right to shoot you down."

"Head on is what I know." Ben replied.

"Kingsley rode in with another marshal." Hollister drawled.

"What? Are you sure?" Emmett asked.

"Well, he's wearin' a badge. That's all I know for sure. That and he's not with Kingsley. He's over at the Casa Espíritus. I heard he's sweet on Verónica."

"That Mexican cantina? The other side of the bridge?" Ben asked.

Emmett nodded. "Why didn't he go to the saloon with Kingsley?"

"They was arguing when they got to town, but I wasn't close enough to hear what they was arguin' about. I don't think they like each other much. Might just shoot each other if you give 'em time." Hollister said.

"We need to use this to our advantage." Emmett said.

"We get a chance to talk to this new marshal, might just convince him to our side." Ben said.

"Might." Emmett said. "Hollister, you stay here and make sure Red Jack stays put while Ben and I go take care of business."

"Mr. Perkins. I wish you'd leave it alone. You haven't seen Kingsley in action. That man's a killer." Hollister said in his southern drawl.

"Can't be helped Hollister. I can't raise my family in this territory with men like Kingsley running wild. Ben, let's go talk to this other marshal. See what he has to say." Emmett said.

"Lead the way." Ben replied with the quiet determination of a man who is no stranger to battle.

Not long after Ben and Emmett had left, Hollister had just settled in when he heard a thump from outside the barn. Rising to his feet, he called out "Mr. Perkins? Is that you?"

"No, old man. This is Marshal Kingsley." The big man stepped into the barn shutting the door behind him.

Hollister gasped and stepped back almost falling because of his crutch.

"The real question is, are you going to die for this no account outlaw? Or are you going to be smart and step aside?" Kingsley said.

"God damn you Perkins." Red Jack yelled from behind the door. "I told you this was a bad idea, but did you listen? No."

Hollister kept his hands far from his holstered pistol, and hobbled out of the way. "No sir Marshal. You will not get any problem from me. No sir, none at all."

"Open the door." Kingsley ordered him.

"Yes sir Marshal." Hollister hobbled over and kicked the wedge from the door, swinging it open.

"Get out here Red Jack." Kingsley ordered.

"Why? You're just going to shoot me. I think you need to come in here." Red Jack replied.

Kingsley picked up a singletree and entered the tack room. Red Jack wasn't tied, but he didn't stand a chance against the marshal even without a bum leg. Kingsley's first blow knocked the outlaw to the floor, the second knocked him out and opened a gash in his scalp.

Kingsley kept the singletree and dragged Red Jack out of the room into the barn. Hollister stood there watching wide-eyed and mute.

"Go get me a rope." Kingsley ordered.

"Yes sir marshal." Hollister went back into the tack room and returned with a coiled length of rope.

"Tie his feet and make it good." Kingsley said.

Hollister bent to the task.

"Give me the other end." Kingsley said. "Come with me." He then dragged the unconscious man out of the barn by his tied feet and headed for the big cottonwood at the edge of town. It was all Hollister could do to keep up.

Approaching the big tree, Kingsley sized up the lower branches. Only one remotely would do for the job at hand. He dragged Red Jack under it.

"Untie his feet." Kingsley ordered Hollister.

"Yes sir Marshal sir."

"Give me the rope."

Hollister had never seen anybody tie a hangman's knot so he had no way to properly judge what he witnessed. How he described it later was the marshal's hands took on a life of their own as they sculpted the perfect hangman's noose. Kingsley picked up the singletree and tied the other end of the rope to it. Then stepping away a few feet, he gave it a mighty toss up and over the limb. It was the weight of the singletree and his strength that got it through the foliage.

Even Hollister knew what was coming next. Kingsley put the noose over Jack Almer's head and tightened it making sure the knot was along his spine. Then he started pulling up the rope until the outlaw was swinging barely an inch above mother earth, his toes kicking up a bit of dust. Kingsley used Jack's red hair to pull his head back so he could see the life drain from the man, enjoying the moment of death. Red Jack Almer never regained consciousness and died quickly. "*Ahhhhhh!*" The lawman made a strange sound.

"Did you say something Marshal?" Hollister asked.

"Five out of six. That deserves a drink. Think I'll go visit that Mexican gal Meade is so interested in." The self-satisfied tone coming from this flawed lawman would stay with Hollister for the rest of his life.

Emmett Perkins

When they left the barn, Ben and Emmett stayed off Main Street keeping to the back yards and passing a number of outhouses on the path they took. The underbrush had mostly been cleared within the town, but not in the gulch itself. The two men worked their horses down one side using narrow animal trails. There was still water running at the bottom, but only a trickle compared to the night of the storm. Ben's black wanted to stay when they reached the water forcing him to use his spurs, something he almost never did.

It was morning, but many of the Mexicans living on this side of town had been up since before dawn. The cantina was on high ground amongst a stand of huge cottonwoods. Its thick adobe walls and low roof made it appear a natural part of its surroundings. The two men tied off at the hitch rail under a cottonwood and walked in.

It was noticeably cooler inside the cantina. Ben went first, his pistol drawn and resting easy in his hand. The gun was cocked and ready to fire, but he kept his finger off the trigger. Just inside the front door, they paused to let their eyes adjust. They were standing in a small lobby used for coats, hats, and gun belts of the establishment's customers.

Just beyond was the main room of the cantina, filled with tables and a long bar against one wall. It was empty, but they could hear voices coming from the back of the cantina. Emmett tapped his chest and took the lead, heading towards the voices. He made a beeline across the cantina and stopped at a curtain covering the doorway leading to the kitchen area. Ben took a different route across the room as much as possible and covered his rear. From behind the curtain, they hear a woman and a child talking. Emmett waits for the kid to leave then eases past the curtain.

"Buenos días, Roni. It's been a long time." Emmett said.

"Emmett, you shouldn't be here. Mucho dangerous. That loco lawman is in town asking about you." The woman was edgy.

"Why is that? How did he know about me?" Emmett asked.

"I have told him about your telegraph." The man was sitting having a plate of beans and a tortilla at a table in the corner of the kitchen. Emmett couldn't see him until he was all the way in the room.

"Who're you?" Emmett asked.

"U.S. Marshal Peter Meade. My friends call me Pete. I was in Jerome when your telegraph came in. The governor dispatched me down here to take charge of Red Jack Almer. You got him jailed somewhere?" Meade was a lean man about the same height as Ben, but not as broad shouldered. Time spent under the Arizona sun had turned his skin into old leather. Gray streaked his thick mustache. "You want to tell your friend to come where I can see him. He's making me nervous."

"Ben, come on in and meet Marshal Pete Meade." Emmett said.

Ben slipped in and tipped his hat. "Marshal." He put himself where he could cover both Meade and the kitchen's two doors.

"Roni, this is my partner, Ben Banyon. Ben this is Verónica Rodriquez, proprietor of the Casa Espíritus." Emmett said.

"Pleased to make your acquaintance, ma'am." Ben tipped his hat to her.

"Verónica Rodriquez de la Peña de Ybarra, but you can call me Roni. I suppose this one's married?" She asked Emmett.

"Afraid so." Emmett replied.

"Too bad..." Veronica wasn't young anymore, but still beautiful. Slim and voluptuous, she had pulled her great abundance of pitch black hair off her neck and piled it high on her head. A low cut bodice showed plenty of cleavage.

"What's the matter with you two? You act as if you're expecting trouble." Meade said scooping up beans with a piece of tortilla..

"What do you know about Kingsley?" Emmett asked.

"Deputy Kingsley? Good lawman, always gets his man. In fact, he brought down the Almer gang, all except Red Jack and now, thanks to you, we have him."

"He murdered one of your deputies and several other people these last few weeks. And he attacked Ben's wife. The man isn't a good lawman, like you think." Emmett said.

Meade chewed on a bite of beans and said. "I don't put much stock in the accusations of him murdering Deputy Watt. He explained it to me much different than what you told in your telegram. Tom shot Deputy Watt then tried to kill Kingsley. It's Tom Almer who shot Levi, not Kingsley."

Emmett nodded. "I thought he would say something like that. And it's his word against... who? They're all dead, all except Red Jack."

"I don't care about that. I want Kingsley because he hurt my wife." Ben said.

Meade nodded. "He told me about that too. Said she was home alone and looking for companionship. He only did what comes natural to a man. She wanted it so that's not rape. That is, unless you have some proof?"

The change in Ben was immediate. "Is this proof enough?" He flipped the badge to Meade who plucked it out of the air.

"It's a deputy's badge. So what?" He looked at the piece of tin. The dark red could be dried blood, and it was in a similar pattern to what he had given Kingsley.

"It was clutched in my wife's hand." Ben said.

"And I suppose she's accusing Kingsley as well?" When Ben didn't reply, Meade frowned then asked softly. "Is she deceased?"

"Jossy was beaten and left for dead." Emmett said for Ben. "But she's alive."

"I tracked what happened at my place and know for a fact what Kingsley did. He's not going to get away with it by hiding behind any badge." Ben spoke softly, but intensely.

Meade knew that look in Ben's eyes. "Son, you don't want to shoot a Deputy U.S. Marshal and you sure don't want to brace me. Very bad for your health."

"Whoa, whoa, whoa." Emmett stepped between the two men

and got in Ben's face. "What are you doing Ben? Meade here is not the enemy."

Ben frowned and looked away in confusion. "You're right. My apologies Marshal Meade."

Meade shrugged. "I can understand your frustration. If what you say is true, Kingsley is a bad apple."

Emmett turned on Meade. "If we're not liars? Listen and try to keep up. Kingsley is a cold blooded killer and rapist."

Meade didn't like his tone, but let it pass. "The law can't just take your word. It needs proof."

"You some kind of lawyer or something?" Emmett asked.

"I'm a lawman. I uphold the law and the law says you must have proof to put a man in jail."

"What about Neally? Kingsley cut his throat." Emmett said.

"Kingsley says your wife had already done that when he arrived." Meade said.

"And I suppose she dragged a grown man from our house too? She weighs less than eight stone and beaten half dead." Ben's voice cracked.

"Your wife needs to file a complaint." Meade said.

"So it's her word against his?" Emmett said.

"Certainly looks that way." Meade replied. "Now take me to Red Jack. The governor is anxious to get his hands on that sorry bag of shit."

Ben shook his head. "Not until you at least talk to my wife."

Meade frowned "That's not why I'm here Mr. Banyon. The governor sent me to bring Red Jack Almer to Prescott where he will stand trial for the murder of the governor's daughter. I don't have time or the authority to do anything about Kingsley, even if I wanted to."

"So you don't want to? Is that it? The rape of a farmer's wife is simply not worthy of your time?" Ben was getting all worked up again.

"No, no, that's not what I mean..." Then he stopped and looked at Ben. making up his mind, he nodded. "How far's your place?"

"Four miles upstream of Sycamore on the Verde." Emmett answered for him.

"Then let's go hear her statement and I will file it in Prescott when I get back. If Kingsley's guilty, he'll be punished. Then I want Almer and no more stalling. Agreed?"

Ben and Emmett nod.

To Ben, the ride seemed an eternity. The last time he'd seen Jossy, she was in bad shape and drugged up. The little he had heard from the townsfolk was encouraging. She was eating well and talking if they was to be believed.

Angus had just finished milking Buttercup the cow and was on his way back to the house when he heard the horses. Stopping on the porch, he could see three riders approaching.

"**Mary, Jossy, we have company**." He called through the open door. "*It's Ben!*" He set the milk bucket down out of harms way.

Mary came out the door first, and stood by her husband as the men rode up. "Ben! Good to see you! Jossy, come on out and give this man a hug before I beat you to it."

Jossy stepped from the house hesitantly, not yet believing that Ben had come home to her. "Oh god..." Tears rolled down her checks. "Is this a dream?"

Ben came off his horse before it was stopped letting the reins fall, bounded up the steps and swept her into his arms. Their lips fused together. It was Jossy who broke it off and pushed Ben away. "Don't you ever leave me again. Never."

Ben nodded and stepped towards her. "Never."

Jossy threw herself back in his arms and looked up at him, her face still bruised and cuts scabbed over. "Did you kill him?" she whispered.

Ben shook his head no.

"Mrs. Banyon? My name is Marshal Meade. I would like to hear your side of the story, if I could?"

Jossy looked from Ben to Meade and back. "My side of the story?" Raw fear made her voice tremble. She turned back to Ben. "So he's still out there?"

"If you mean Deputy Kingsley, he's in Sycamore, Mrs. Banyon." Meade said.

"Oh god." Jossy put both hands over her mouth and looked ready to collapse at any moment.

"Jossy, you must tell him everything. Marshal Meade promised to help, but only if he knows everything." Ben didn't like the sound of that after hearing it come out of his own mouth.

"Everything?" Jossy didn't like it much either.

Meade nodded. "It's the only way."

Jossy frowned, but nodded.

"Why don't we go inside. I got a pot of coffee and there's stew." Mary suggested.

Once inside, Jossy and Meade went to sit by the fire leaving the table to Ben, Emmett and Angus. While Mary busied herself in the kitchen, they put their heads together and quietly swapped stories of the past week. In the main room, Meade pulled pen and paper from his saddlebag and diligently wrote down every word Jossy told him. He read it back at the end and she signed it.

Getting up, Jossy came into the kitchen followed by Meade. "I told him everything Ben, just like you wanted. I hope it don't get us both killed."

"I'll talk to Kingsley before I leave and make sure he won't bother you folks. It may take several weeks to see any action so be patient and let the system work." Meade said.

"Did you believe her or is Jossy a liar too?" Ben asked.

"I never called you a liar. And yes, I believe her. Marshal Kingsley needs to be stopped. I will let the governor know when I see him and I'm sure he will agree, but now I want Almer. Take me to him."

Ben and Emmett stood up.

"What? Are you leaving again so soon." Jossy looked ready to collapse at the thought.

Ben put his arms around her. "Just for an hour or so."

"I can take care of it Ben. You stay here with your wife. She needs you more right now." Emmett offered.

Ben shook his head. "I'm seeing this through."

"Kingsley said he would kill you if you come after him. Don't do it Ben. Please stay here with me." Jossy clutched at him, the fear radiating from her in waves like heat off a bonfire.

"We won't see Kingsley ma'am. I'll pick up my prisoner and be on my way. These men can go about their business." Meade said.

"We'll stay with you 'till Ben gets back." Mary said

Angus nodded. "Aye lass. As long as it takes."

Jossy stood with her arms folded across her chest as if shielding her heart from pain. "You better come right home, you hear?"

"Yes ma'am, straight home." Ben hugged and kissed her as she stood there rigid and unmoving. He stepped up on the black, tipped his hat to Angus and Mary, and galloped after the other two men.

Jossy stood unmoving until Ben was out of sight, tears rolled slowly down her cheeks.

Emmett was talking with Meade as he caught up with them. "Red Jack is in the back of a barn at the far edge of town. I have a man guarding him."

"Good. Let's ride." Meade put the spurs to his mount and soon they were coming over the last rise and looking down at Sycamore shimmering peaceful in the afternoon sun.

Coming into town, Emmett was the first to notice. "Where's everybody?"

Main Street was empty, not a soul to be seen anywhere. "Let's keep to the outskirts. Follow me." Emmett led them off on a side trail, not much more than a walking path weaving its way among the shacks and cabins and other buildings. Still nobody in sight when they arrived at the barn. Stepping down, the men approached the closed barn doors cautiously, their hands resting on their guns.

Emmett motioned Ben to one side and he swung open one door. Ben drew his gun then darted in, moving away from the open door. Emmett followed, but going the other way. Meade hung back for a moment then followed them in.

Besides the partially opened main door, the side door leading to the corral was wide open and the shutter to the loft brought in more light. Looking down the length of the barn, the storage room was empty. Red Jack was gone. No sign of Hollister either.

Ben started a sweep of the floor finding an abundance of tracks inside the barn. Some old, some new. The real trick is to find the sign you care about. He held up his hand when Emmett and Meade started to approach the storage room.

"Stop right there. Let me read the sign." Ben moved to cut them off and pointed to a clear print in the thick dust. "That's Kingsley's boot. The blood leads from the tack room out the door, but I don't think he shot Red Jack." Ben followed the track to the storeroom. "Kingsley went inside and dragged Red Jack out. Why would he do that if he killed him?"

"OK, so he's alive. Any idea where he would have taken Almer?" Pete asked.

Ben and Emmett looked at each other for a moment, then Emmett said. "The Tumbleweed Saloon unless I miss my guess. I thought I would use Red Jack as bait to draw Kingsley in and now it looks like he may be thinking to do the same."

"Why would he do that? Why not just kill Red Jack and take off?" Meade asked.

"You're thinking like a lawman chasing an outlaw. Kingsley is no outlaw." Emmett replied.

"He'll be waiting for us." Ben said.

They left their horses there and walked towards the center of town. Taking to the boardwalk, they stopped outside the little cafe where they had eaten the night before. The Tumbleweed Saloon was across the way. Main Street was wide here with a good sized cottonwood to one side.

That's when Ben noticed the body hanging from one of its limbs. "Marshal, you'll find your prisoner under yonder cottonwood."

Turning to look. "Oh damn." Meade said.

Emmett took it hardest. "I promised him a fair trial."

Meade shook his head. "Chances are, that was how he would have ended. Kingsley just deprived the governor of his show."

"I don't think that was an accident." Ben said.

"You're probably right." He turned back to stare across Main at the saloon. "Let me go in and talk to him first. He may be in there waiting for me." Meade said.

"Sure, and after he confesses to rape and murder, the two of you will ride off to Prescott where he will go peacefully to the gallows." Ben said.

"Pete, you go in there alone and Kingsley will kill you for sure." Emmett added.

"Well, aren't you two a breath of sunshine." Pete said.

Just then, Otis and Quinn came out of the saloon and stood on the porch. It took only a moment for them to see Ben, Emmett and Pete. Otis waved and the two of them hustled across Main Street. Otis was carrying his sawed off shotgun, and Quinn was wearing a gun for the first time in memory.

"You boys have your work cut out for you. Kingsley done hung Red Jack Almer." Otis said.

"And he's waitin' for you at Casa Espíritus." Quinn said to the marshal.

"Why the Casa?" Pete asked, but he already knew the answer.

"Don't know, but he said to tell ya it's payback time." Quinn replied.

When he hesitated, Ben said. "Come on Pete, spill the beans."

"So why's he going after Verónica?" Otis asked. "He made it plenty clear that she was why he was going there."

Pete said. "Damn. I told him I liked her."

"He's a rabid dog." Quinn said. "Completely crazy. I seen it during the war. Men would become possessed of some evil spirit and do unspeakable things."

Pete was in a full sweat. If everything he had learned about Kingsley was true, and he now fully believed it was, someone he cared deeply for was in the path of this so-called rabid dog. Kingsley had taken it to a whole new level and there was no turning back.

"It's past time to kill the bastard." Ben said.

"Where's Hollister?" Emmett asked.

"Ah, he went with Kingsley. You got to understand him, Mr. Perkins. He ain't got much backbone. He tends to bend with whatever wind comes by." Otis said.

Emmett shook his head. "Well, he's fired when I see him."

"I'm sure he knows that, Mr. Perkins." Otis replied.

Quinn snorted scornfully. "Really? I seriously doubt that. He thinks he can talk his way out of the biggest pile of shit."

"You sure you know how to use that?" Emmett pointed at the gun on Quinn's hip.

"What? Oh, yes sir. I was a sergeant in the 16th Illinois Volunteer Cavalry. That's where I learned horses." Quinn said.

"And you lost your foot fighting for the south?" Emmett asked Otis.

"At Bull Run, Mr. Perkins." Otis replied.

"Ain't we a motley crew." Emmett said.

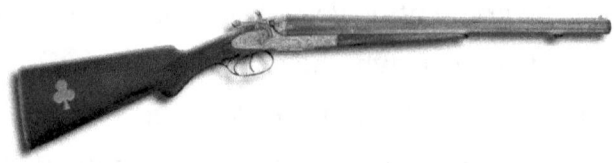

Pete Meade

The five men rode into the yard outside the Casa Espíritus and stopped at the water trough under the broad limbs of another old cottonwood. The horses buried their muzzles in the cool water, their ears flicking at the flies buzzing about them. A young Mexican boy emerged from the cantina carrying a tin pail and headed toward the shacks down the hill. The bright sun overhead promised another hot, lazy afternoon in Sycamore.

"I want you men to stay here." Pete said. "This is not your fight."

"The hell you say. I'm going in with you." Ben said.

"It's a free country marshal and we have business inside the cantina." Emmett pulled his new rifle from its saddle boot. "You might as well get used to it."

"Humph. One more thing, there's a letter in my saddlebag that needs to be sent. It's the report Jossy gave me and I have added some thoughts of my own. It needs to get into the hands of the governor." Pete said.

"You'll give it to him personally right after we take care of

Kingsley." Emmett said.

Pete shrugged. "Just in case."

"Don't you fret none. I'll make sure it gets there." Quinn said.

Pete nodded at Quinn. "Thanks. You watch the front and stay with the horses."

"Alright." Quinn nodded approvingly. That was a plan he could get behind.

Pete then turned to Otis. "You go around back and shoot Kingsley if you see him. You let him shoot first and Sycamore will need a new barkeep."

Otis nodded and limped off at a good pace with his shotgun in hand.

Pete led Emmett and Ben across the yard. The old Mexican who worked at the cantina had just finished lighting the oil lamp outside the front door as Pete, Ben and Emmett walked up. "Bueno noches, señors. Welcome to the Casa Espíritus." White men with guns made him unhappy which made him very unhappy today.

"Looks like everything is quiet around here, huh amigo?" Pete asked.

"Ah, si, pretty good."

"Is Marshal Kingsley in the back?" Pete asked.

"Ah nooooo, señor." He stretched out the reply while shaking his head. "I don't think so. Nobody here."

Pete thought that must be a lie. "You sure about that?"

Ben grabbed the old man by his shirt and confronted him, nose to nose. "We know he's here, now tell us where he's at."

Fear passed over the old man's face like an Arizona rain cloud during monsoon. "If I tell you then he kill me and if I don't then you beat me up."

Emmett laid his hand on Ben's arm. "Let it go. We'll find him."

"Your name is Elisio, right?" Pete asked. He recognized him from earlier visits to the Casa.

"Si. Senorita Verónica hired me last year."

"As I recall, when nobody else would? What are you, seventy? Yet she took you in and gave you a job. Just look at you. New shirt, new pants, clean washed, well fed, now she's in trouble and needs your help." Pete leaned down and spoke softly. "She needs you to step up. Tell us where they are."

Elisio was nervous, avoiding Pete's eyes. "Marshal Kingsley wouldn't hurt the senorita." He said it more to convince himself then them.

"I think you know that's not true." Emmett said.

The Mexican shifted his gaze from Emmett to Ben then to Pete. "Senorita Verónica herself told me not to tell you."

"What's that? Why would she do that?" Ben asked.

"Because she knows Kingsley... Knows what he is." Emmett said turning to look intently at Pete. "And so do you, right Marshal Meade? You know exactly what Kingsley is, always did, yet you haven't done anything about it. Why's that?"

Pete stood silent for a moment, but his expression told the story. "The governor said every territory needs an enforcer, someone not afraid to get their hands dirty. He has visions of Arizona becoming a state and thinks Kingsley is useful. I now see now how wrong that was."

Ben grabbed Pete and pushed the marshal against the wall.

"Then my wife is just collateral damage? All them people he killed? Just the price for statehood? Is that what this is all about? Politics?"

Emmett again laid his hand on Ben's arm. "Easy Ben. Pete isn't to blame. He follows orders. Right Marshal? You had orders to come down here and pull Kingsley out of the shit house again. I'm curious, how many times have you done that?"

Ben kept Pete pinned against the wall and now they stared at each other, up close and personal. Pete spoke first. "I'm sincerely sorry about your wife and there's only one thing I can do for those Kingsley murdered and wronged, and that's to stop him before he does it again."

"The governor ain't going to like it."

"The governor can kiss my ass." Pete said.

"What made you change your mind?" Ben asked.

"He's got Verónica and then there's your wife."

Ben frowned. "What about her?"

"She's quite a woman. Jossy convinced me that this had gone on too long and it was time to put a stop to Kingsley. Now, are you going to let me do my job or not?"

Ben let Pete go and stepped back.

"Good." Pete straightened his shirt and went to confront the old Mexican. "Senorita Verónica is my friend and I want to help her so I'm going to ask you one last time, Elisio. Where did Kingsley take her?" When the old man started to hesitate, Pete held up a finger and wagged it at him in warning. "*Me dicen, Elisio.*"

The old man walked outside the cantina and pointed towards the adobe shacks and assorted businesses on the south side of

Sycamore. "They went to the Palacio de Placer."

"That figures." Pete began walking back down the hill towards the horses. "Come on. No time to waste."

"What's the Palacio Placer?" Ben asked matching pace with the marshal.

"Palacio de Placer, or Pleasure Palace, is a Mexican whorehouse. Should've known Kingsley would head for it. I'm sure he feels right at home." Pete replied.

"Stay here." Pete called out to Quinn in passing. The liveryman patted his gun and nodded without one thought to ask where they were going.

The Pleasure Palace turned out to be an old hotel. Its thick adobe walls was cracked and large chunks of the outside plaster missing. If it ever had any paint on it, the Arizona sun had long since dried it out and turned it to dust. Now it was well on its way to doing the same to the wood and dirt underneath.

The lobby, where the cowboys and miners picked their whore, was dim and smelled of booze and sweat. What you could see of the red carpet was faded and worn, the furniture in the lobby shabby and dusty, the window drapes torn and threadbare, but at least it was cool inside.

A number of fallen angels lounged about the room and those closest to the door got up when the three came in. They approached the men.

"Buscando un buen tiempo?" The tall one said while giving Ben the eye.

"What'd she say?" Ben asked.

"She's asking if you're looking for a good time. Más tarde, quizá, senorita." Pete replied.

"If you're not looking for girls, why are you here?" Coming down the stairs was an older lady, matronly, and in charge.

Pete faced her. "Pardon us ma'am. We're looking for Marshal Kingsley. Is he here?"

"Si. What do you want with him? I won't tolerate any shooting in my place. The last time Marshal Kingsley was here, I lost two lamps, a bed and my dog. I don't want any trouble."

"Ma'am, the governor will see to it you are properly reimbursed now tell us which room he's in." Pete said.

"I won't hold my breath. He's in the last room on the right." She pointed over her shoulder up the stairs.

"Emmett, you stay here with the ladies and we'll go up and invite him down for a talk." Pete said for the matron's benefit.

Emmett smiled. "Ladies, I think we should all adjourn to the kitchen."

Ben and Pete started for the stairs as Emmett herded the women into the kitchen area in the back of the first floor.

With pistols drawn, Pete and Ben stepped softly up the stairs and down the hallway. They heard the distant ringing of a church bell.

There were three doors on the right and four on the left. A large window at the far end of the hallway had heavy drapes that kept the sunlight outside. Inside was lit with coal oil lamps hung on the wall half way between each door. Black soot streaked the wall behind each lamp and across the ceiling above them.

"Take that side." Pete said softly then turned the knob on the door pushing it open. Carefully looking inside while not exposing too much, they determined that the room was occupied, but not by Kingsley.

Beyond a tumbled bed, a young woman stood in front of a mirror, dressed only in a corset, but completely undisturbed by the intrusion. She watched their reflection in the mirror as she went on tending a black eye and bruised face. Her right eye was not only a deep shade of blue, it was swollen completely shut.

Ben frowned and went to her. Just like Jossy, her face was cut and mangled on the right side, her right eye the only one damaged. Ben whispered. "Kingsley did this, didn't he?"

At the mention of Kingsley, her one clear eye, the left, clouded over and she tilted her head meaningfully towards the next room.

Going back out to the hallway, Ben went to the next door and opened it. Again, he made sure he wouldn't get shot before stepping inside. Another whore was relaxing on the bed. A look of interest swept over her face when she got a good look at Ben. Ben put a finger to his lips and moved around the room searching it.

Pete didn't wait for Ben, but started down the hallway toward the third door. He heard a strange noise. *"Ahhhhhh!"* He crept closer to the door and reached for the knob. As he swung it open, careful to not expose too much of himself to anyone inside the room, he seen Kingsley over by the bed holding that damned shotgun. He ducked back, but was too late.

The shotgun blast exploded through the wall at his back hitting him heart high. The violent impact of so much mass drove him across the hallway and smashed him against the wall. He fell to the floor mortally wounded.

"Ahhhhhh!" Another kill. Kingsley was drunk with power. Killing people was too easy, or maybe he just had a talent for it. He moved to the doorway.

Ben came charging into the hallway. Plaster dust was so thick that when Kingsley pulled the trigger on the remaining barrel, he missed, blowing away part of the door jamb Ben had just came through.

Kingsley growled, an animal sound that came from deep in his chest. He never missed. He stood there in denial a moment too long.

Ben fired two quick shots, the first one hitting Kingsley's shotgun right where it breaks down, the second cutting empty air where he had been.

Kingsley ducked back into the room and dropped the damaged shotgun. He ran through the French doors and out onto the balcony. At full speed and without any hesitation, the marshal vaulted over the railing to a wagon parked in the street below. He had planned his escape route carefully. From there, he dropped to the ground and ran to the corner of the building across from the entrance to the whorehouse. Using it as cover, he watched and waited.

Back in the hallway, Ben slowed down his thoughts and assessed the situation. Marshal Meade was dead and Kingsley done it. Ben was determined, but it wouldn't do anybody any good if he got himself killed too. It wasn't until he let in the image of his beautiful Jossy laying beaten and bruised in their bed that real anger surged through him. He did what all his training had taught him to do, he cocked his pistol and attacked his enemy head on. Ben burst into the room ready to fire nearly tripping on the shotgun laying on the floor. The room was empty except for someone lying on the bed. It was Verónica. She lay on her back staring at the ceiling with eyes wide open, her throat slit ear to ear. Blood soaked the sheets under her and dripped to the floor, but no Kingsley. He was gone. One look at the balcony and he knew where. Ben stepped into the hallway ayelled at the top of his lungs. "OUTSIDE."

Emmett barely heard him over the crying and carrying on of the women. He went to the front door and opened it cautiously. He was greeted with a bullet smacking into the wood next to his face throwing out splinters. Emmett jerked back, but he had seen where the shot came from. The thin puff of white smoke gave Kingsley's position away. The rancher returned fire, his bullets gouging holes in the adobe close to Kingsley. The roar from his new rifle did get the marshal's attention, but it was the bullets that forced him back. Then to Emmett's utter astonishment, Ben landed on the street almost in front of him.

Ben dropped from the balcony landing hard on the dirt street next to it, falling short of the wagon. Pain knifed through his ankle. The wagon provided him poor cover. He was exposed here and needed to move, but as soon as he started to put weight on it, the ankle gave way. Pain washed over him in waves.

Kingsley took notice of what had happened to Ben and cackled loud enough for both men to hear. When he leaned out from the corner to draw a bead on Ben, Emmett levered shot after shot, pounding the adobe near Kingsley's head driving him back, but the lawman still managed to get a couple shots off.

"Get in here, Ben." Emmett called out.

Ben gritted his teeth and surged to his feet, stumbling forward to throw himself through the whorehouse door. He landed with a thud on the garish red carpet. Emmett kicked the heavy door shut.

"You crazy? What possessed you to jump off a building?" Emmett noticed the blood. "You're hit."

"Just a scratch." Ben used his bandana to tie it off. It was a skin wound that hurt like hell fire itself, but otherwise, no muscle damage. It was the ankle that worried him more. He rubbed it which did help. The pain wasn't so bad. "I'll be fine. Where's Kingsley?"

"Across the street beyond that corner where we can't see him, but I'll bet my saddle he's on the move." Emmett said. "That way is a little church then the gulch."

"Did you hit him?" Ben asked.

Emmett was reloading his rifle. "Don't think so. Did you?"

Ben shook his head.

"The bastard has nine lives." Emmett looked over at Ben. "What about Pete?"

Ben shook his head. "Took the shotgun square in the back."

"Damn. I was getting to like the son of a bitch."

"There's more." Ben said. "Your friend, Veronica, is dead. Throat slit."

Emmett didn't say anything, but his hardened expression spoke volumes.

"Let's go out the back door and come at him from another direction." Ben said.

Emmett nodded and Ben led the way noticeably limping, but shaking it off. Ben was greatly relieved that it wasn't worse, much worse. The two men moved quickly through the kitchen area, telling the ladies there to stay put. Once outside, it didn't take them long to determine that Kingsley was gone. Darting from one bit of cover to the next, they moved forward cautiously.

Coming to the edge of a building, Emmett motioned with his gun then peeked around the corner.

Not far away was a small adobe church, a whitewashed one-room building with a heavy wooden front door. Tied outside the church was an old swayback mare hitched to a wagon. Nervous at all the shooting, she was snorting and moving about, her eyes wide in fear.

Ben spotted him first. "Behind the wagon."

Kingsley heard him and knew he'd been seen. He fired hitting the corner of the building and forcing Ben to duck back. The marshal abandoned the wagon and bolted through the front door of the church.

Ben hadn't been looking at that moment, but Emmett had. He yelled over to him. "In the church." Emmett motioned with his rifle that he would cover him.

Without wasting more time, Ben flat out ran towards the church keeping the wagon between him and the door, and staying out of Emmett's line of fire. The mare fought her halter ropes on his approach, rolling her eyes in fear. Ben moved slower. "Easy girl." He ran his hands along the horse calming her. Emmett joined him behind the wagon arriving out of breath. "You stay here." Ben said then ran to the church pressing his back against the thick adobe wall next to the front door. He waited a moment then slipped inside.

"That's either bravery or crazy, hard to tell the difference." Emmett muttered.

Ben moved away from the doorway and waited for his eyes to adjust. An impressive display of candles were burning across the front behind the pulpit providing the only light in the church.

The congregation, mostly women, knelt in their flicker, heads draped in black mantillas. They rolled their rosary beads in their hands while the parish priest officiated in Latin, of which Ben understood not one word.

A commotion up front drew his attention. Kingsley was heading for the back door when the priest stepped in his way. The marshal shot him through the heart. He was dead before he hit the floor.

"Ahhhhhh!" Ben clearly heard the strange sound.

Then all hell broke lose. The parishioners jumped to their feet and rushed for the front door intent on getting away from the gun at the back door. The swarming confusion only lasted a few seconds, but it was long enough for Kingsley to escape.

There was several women that didn't run. Ben found them crying over the body of their priest. He paused, but they never looked up, just rocked back and forth chanting their grief.

Ben moved to the back door and opened it slightly, peeking out. Not seeing any sign of Kingsley, he opened it more and planned his next move. Mescal Gulch was not far and he assumed Kingsley had gone there. It offered cover and a way to put some distance between them without being seen. He didn't like the open ground between here and there.

No help for it. Ben rushed from the back door of the church and sprinted across the space towards the relative safety of the gulch. He seen movement to his right at the edge of the gully and instinct made him dive left away from it. The move saved his life. The Colt's muzzle flash seemed absurdly close and huge.

"Damn!" Kingsley roared when he missed.

Ben was still caught in the open. He scrambled on the hands

and knees towards the nearest cover, an old privy that hadn't been used in years. Its ancient wood planks offered very little protection, but it was better than nothing.

Then from the corner of the church, Emmett opened fire with that rifle driving Kingsley down into the gully preventing him from shooting Ben.

Breathing hard more from emotion rather than exertion, Ben waved at Emmett and sprinted the final few feet to the gulch then dropped out of sight. He was uphill from where Kingsley had been so he found a spot behind a rocky outcropping and paused to listen. Yes, he could hear movement through the thick brush further down the wash.

From this position, Ben had eyes on the both sides of the gulch all the way to the river. A flume carrying water to the Verde Foundry towered twenty feet overhead. The brush had been cleared beneath it allowing Ben to see Kingsley when he emerged from hiding. He was over fifty yards away, a long shot with a pistol. Ben fired repeatedly at the marshal as he ran towards the flume hitting him once in the thigh sending him to the ground.

Kingsley crawled the final few feet to cover under the flume, ducking behind the nearest support beam. When Emmett opened up on him with that rifle from further down the gulch, Kingsley realized he had no place to run and a bum leg even if there was. He fired back at Emmett then at Ben, reloaded and kept firing knowing full well he was in a tight spot.

The wooden beam wasn't much cover. Kingsley took a pistol bullet in the shoulder then a rifle bullet tore into the beam sending wood fragments into his scalp and forehead. Blood filled his eyes making it difficult to reload or see what he was shooting at. He looked around for a way out, but there was none. For the first time in his life, fear crept into his brain setting it on fire.

"WHO ARE YOU?" Kingsley roared in frustration. A bullet nipped the heel of his boot right off. Another hit him in his already wounded shoulder, this one smashing bone.

Then systemically, Emmett started hitting the support beam with his new rifle ripping away chunks, weakening it bit by bit. He reloaded and continued firing, cutting it down like a lumberjack harvesting a tree. Laying low on the ground, Kingsley heard the final splintering as the weight of the water-filled plume high overhead exceeded the strength of the damaged beam. He rolled over and looked up as it began to fall.

"NOOOO!" Kingsley screamed and tried to roll away. Water went everywhere on impact and the marshal was buried under tons of soggy wood.

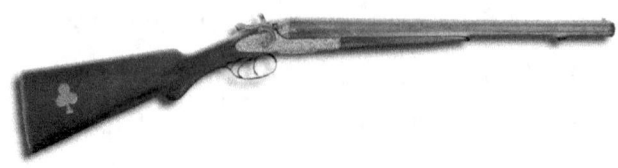

Frank Kingsley

Sunset had been spectacular. Ben and Jossy had gone up on the plateau to see it and had come home ready for supper. Ben was seated at the table watching Jossy putter around the kitchen fixing the meal. The cook stove was all they needed to heat the house against the night chill. It was a cozy warm evening, a stark contrast to the long ordeal they had just lived through. It would be some time before either of them could talk about what had happened, if ever.

Jossy filled Ben's coffee cup and set the pot back on the stove. She removed a pan of biscuits from the oven and set them on the stove beside the pot. She got the ham from the cupboard and began cutting thin slices from it with her favorite butcher knife. Ben liked ham, scrambled eggs and biscuits.

She worked at the sideboard in front of the window right next to the stove. It was dark outside, but she never noticed the strange reflections on the giant cottonwood tree until it was too late. The fire had started outside the bedroom near the back door and quickly spread to the roof. By the time Ben and Jossy became aware that something was wrong, their house was in flames.

"BEN." Jossy screamed. She stood frozen in the middle of the kitchen with the knife still in her hand.

"Come on. We got to get out of here." Ben pushed her towards the front door. Smoke filled their home and they were coughing when they emerged on the porch. Ben brought Jossy out to the yard well away from the flames. She wasn't doing well at all. It was as if she had gone into a trance, she walked strangely and stared off into the distance not seeing what was right in front of her. Ben shook her. "Jossy, you must help me. We can't let the fire get to the barn. Jossy? Do you hear me?"

"Damn." He turned to go retrieve his guns and other valuables from the inferno, but the dried wooden structure was totally engulfed. It was suicide to attempt it. All Ben could do was stand beside Jossy and watch their home go up in flames.

From the dense shadow cast by the flames behind the big cottonwood at the edge of their yard, Kingsley snarled. "Whore! I told you to not make somethin' of what we done."

Ben wheeled about pulling Jossy behind him, putting himself between her and this bloody apparition that appeared before them.

Blood covered his face, shoulder, and side, and his left arm hung limp and useless. More blood soaked his pants and he moved slowly dragging a leg. Kingsley was in bad shape, but nothing was wrong with the pistol he held in his hand.

"Who'd have thought a farmer's wife would go running their mouth like a common whore. Now every sons-a-bitch between here and Mexico knows." Kingsley pulled himself towards them. "Don't you move or I'll kill you right now." He waved the gun around and kept coming.

"Let Jossy go. This is between us." Ben ignored the command and kept backing them away from the approaching specter.

Kingsley shot Ben in the leg and nodded when he fell to the ground. "Now that's better. I told you to stop moving."

Jossy stood there in shock staring at Kingsley.

"Don't worry, my queen, I ain't killed him, at least not yet. I want him to see what I got in store for you."

"Why are you doing this?" Jossy cried out.

Kingsley said, "I'm going to let you in on a little secret. That girl, the governor's daughter? I done her." He threw back his head and guffawed hysterically, an eerie and unnerving sound coming from a man who never smiled. "Now ain't that justice? I done her and the governor sends *me* to bring in the men *he* thinks done her? Even then, he couldn't make up his mind. First he wanted Almer dead then he wanted me to bring Almer in alive, but I couldn't let that happen. Almer knowed it was me who done her. He was there, but it was me that done her. That weak-kneed piece of shit would a told. He had to die. Just like you have to die."

"You're one miserable bastard." Ben moaned and sat up. The bullet had missed the bone and gone clear through his thigh muscle. The pain was excruciating. In spite of it, Ben surged to his feet using the intense agony to focus on what he had to do, but pure determination can only take a man so far. He would have fallen, but for Jossy.

"You have no idea how many I've killed, and enjoyed every one. Each life was as sweet as mother's milk." Even over the roar of the fire, they could hear the hammer cock back on Kingsley's pistol. "Life is strong in you, plow boy, so come on, you don't know how I've looked forward to taking it."

Ben lunged across the intervening space, but instead of shooting him, the marshal clubbed Ben with his pistol then stood over him completely devoid of any real emotion. He coldly shot Ben in the leg again, this time hitting bone.

Watching Ben get shot pushed Jossy over the edge. Survival meant everything, nothing else mattered. Her fear evaporated when she realized she still held the butcher knife. Gripping it with both hands, she rushed forward and plunged it into Kingsley's back just below his shoulder blade. His one good arm went limp and he dropped his six-shooter uttering a sound unlike anything she had ever heard, but that son of a bitch still didn't fall. She backed up willing him to go down.

Instead he turned, the butcher knife protruding grotesquely from his back, and looked at her with an insane mixture of shock and utter hostility. He couldn't believe this little slip of a girl had gotten to him. How *dare* she attack *him*.

Jossy backed away. "Die you bastard. Why won't you die?" Her gaze shifted between Kingsley and Ben. Hot tears eroded streaks down her sooty face.

Kingsley shook his head like a wounded bear and started towards her, dragging his leg, the knife itself forming the perfect plug, keeping his blood inside him. He kept coming until she could go no farther, her back to the burning house.

Kingsley coughed and bloody foam gurgled from his mouth. "I could of killed you, but I didn't. You was my Argeia, my Queen of Clubs and the prettiest woman I ever seen on this earth. I wanted you to live so I could come back." He cried out in pain as he reached inside his duster retrieving the deadly little Derringer from its shoulder holster. "But if you ain't mine, you ain't nobody's." He said through the blood and pain.

Ben had pulled himself dragging his shot up leg across the ground to where the marshal's pistol lay. He fired hitting Kingsley in the back.

The marshal dropped the Derringer and stumbled, but still wouldn't go down. "You think this is over? It's only beginning." With his last breath of life, Frank Kingsley, Deputy U.S. Marshal of the Arizona Territory, lumbered at Jossy seemingly intent on grabbing her and plunging them both into the fire. She easily eluded him.

Instead of stopping, Kingsley staggered up the stairs, crossed the porch, and entered the house just as the roof collapsed. Flames engulfed Kingsley and roared a hundred feet into the night sky.

Jossy stood transfixed for a moment by what she had just witnessed. "*Ben!*" She cried out and ran to her husband. Between the two of them, they managed to bandage his leg and stop the bleeding. Then, sitting under the cottonwood, she laid his head in her lap and together, they watched their home burn.

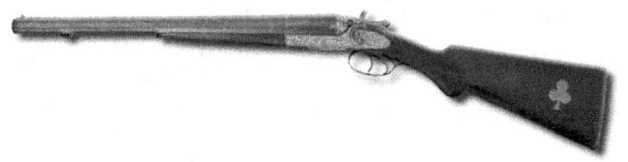

Double Trouble

Fall harvest was behind them and winter was in full swing. Jossy and Mary sat on the porch of the newly rebuilt Banyon home enjoying the last warmth of the day. The house was bigger now, three bedrooms and tight against the cold. The two rockers were new as was the thick woolen blankets spread across their laps. Everything had burned in the fire.

Ma Perkins, Emmett's better half and the best midwife in these parts, came out of the house and said. "I wish you two would come back inside. Them babies won't come any faster if you catch a chill."

"Another minute, Ma." Jossy said. When the midwife started to argue, Jossy frowned and shook her head emphatically at her.

"Fine. I'll have hot soup by the fire when you're ready." Ma went back inside.

Alone once again, Mary looked at her friend. "Honey, you need to stop this worrying. It's all in God's hands. Believe me, this is all part of His plan. This is my miracle baby." She patted her belly. "Besides, you ain't going to be able to tell anything when they are first born."

"I'll know." Jossy said rubbing her own swollen belly.

Mary shook her head. "You already know what I think, you should have talked to Ben about this a long time ago."

"I said *no*." Jossy replied sharply. "You promised not to say anything to Ben." She grew alarmed at the very thought.

Mary reached over and squeezed her hand. "I haven't and I won't, you have my word. He will not find out from me that you ain't sure who the father is." She didn't say what she thought; that Ben was one of the smartest people she had ever met, next to her own husband. And he owned a calendar.

"Good. Let's keep it that way."

"Don't you find this exciting? If it's God's will, we might have our babies on the same day." Mary laid a hand on her extended belly, feeling the baby stir within.

"*Ahhhhhh!*" Jossy grabbed her stomach, then yelled. "MA! SOMETHING'S HAPPENING!"

Ma Perkins was there in a flash. "Lord child, you'd think you was having a baby or something."

Mary grabbed her own stomach and said. "I knew it! I just knew it! This is a miracle! These babies is the will of God! Glory Halleluj*ahhhhhhh!*"

Ma laughed joyfully. "Oh my, now I've seen everything. Two mothers breaking water at the same time. BEN! ANGUS! I'm gonna need some help here."

WATCH FOR THE SEQUEL

Writers Cramp Publishing
http://www.writerscramp.us
editor@writerscramp.us
Amazon, Barnes&Noble, Google, Espresso

About Chuck
The Author's Biography

Let me tell you just a little about myself. My folks were divorced before I was three back when divorce was unheard of. Guess they just couldn't take my incessant howling. No matter. They both loved me and that was all I really cared about at that age. I grew up bouncing between Colorado and Southern California and loving every minute of it. By the time I started high school, I had visited every state west of the Mississippi.

Speaking of high school, mine was in a small town on the Mojave Desert. Counting the occasional tourist, Boron topped out at about 5000 souls, but it wasn't boring. The main part of the town is nestled at the feet of a high-desert volcano-looking mountain with a rocket engine test facility built into its summit. Edwards Air Force Base is just on the other side of it from Boron. You could always tell who was new in town; they flinched every time a sonic boom rattled the windows. The mountain we simply called the Rocket Site and ignored the loud noises. They tested the Saturn 5 engines at the Rocket Site, the ones that took our boys to the moon. Once in a while they would fire them up at night. What a sight. What a noise. Those babies would shake the world in a way impossible to describe. It's something that must be felt and then you will never forget it.

Long story short, after four years in the army mostly in Baumholder, Germany, I went to college and earned a BS in Engineering Mechanics-Aerospace from the University of Wisconsin-Madison and a Masters in Materials Science from Arizona State University. For a while I worked at Space Data/ Orbital Sciences Corporation designing, building, and launching rockets and high altitude weather balloons. I launched rockets from Mexican, Canadian, and American soil. My sounding rockets even launched from the deck of a French frigate. Later, I was the Quality Assurance Manager for Hybrid Design Associates in Tempe. HDA is a small manufacturing company that specializes in harsh-environment electronic assemblies. Among a host of other customers, we built electronic boards for the oil logging industry, Halliburton, Baker Atlas, Pathfinder, etc.

A couple decades ago I was lucky enough to marry the most wonderful woman in the world. We have three kids and five grand-kids with a sixth on the way. I run a small publishing company, Writers Cramp Publishing, and write under my full name, Charles Lee Lesher. My debut novel, Evolution's Child, was selected as 2007's Best of the Moon Fiction by the Lunar Library. You can still buy it, but now it is part of the Republic of Luna series. Evolution's Child has morphed into two Kindle novels, ***Evolution's Child - Earthman*** and ***Evolution's Child - Lunarian***. I know, its weird but what can I say. The creative process is not always as neat as we would like. The third book, ***Revelation's Child***, makes this a trilogy. I am very proud of the eBook versions. Love eBooks on my Fire. (Check out my website at: http://www.charleslesher.com for more info on RoL) You can also buy all three novels in one big bathroom reader, Shadow on the Moon is 500 pages of science fiction excitement.

My latest book is a nonfiction titled ***Out of the Cradle*** on sale as a conventional hardcover and a gorgeous Kindle Fire and Nook Color eBook What I say in the book will bum you out but then it will turn that frown upside down and lift you up. The world is changing and we had better be ready when the big changes come. The biggest change will be energy. Electricity is a key component holding our technological civilization together. What happens when we finally run out of oil and the coal is gone? Don't sweet it, we have the answer and nuclear is not involved, at least, not in your backyard. Buy my book and see how we are doing the impossible.

Chuck's Other Books
Shadow on the Moon

The Republic of Luna is humanities first extraterrestrial nation. Science, genetics and a humanistic society mark it as a target for the powerful Islamic Brotherhood, a global empire with billions of believers. Luna is a world created by pioneers whose only religion is the humane treatment of one another in their common struggle to survive the ultimate hostile environment, space. The heroes that conquered the moon must now defend it. Thankfully, they have a few tricks up their sleeve.

Shadow on the Moon combines *Evolution's Child - Earthman, Evolution's Child - Lunarian, Evolution's Child - Thread*, and *Science of the Republic* into one 500 page Anniversary Print Edition.

ISBN: 978-0-977723-56-0 Paperback

Aldrin Station - Rise of Luna

Aldrin Station is a collection of short stories illuminating Lunarian history from the dawn of mankind to its expansion into space and colonizing the moon. These are stories of the families and individuals that play a role in the Republic of Luna.

ISBN 978-1-938586-00-2 eBook

Science of the Republic

A collection of articles, maps, and tables that help the reader understand the science and technology of the Republic.

ISBN 978-1-938586-04-0 eBook

Evolution's Child - Earthman

Book One: Lazarus Sheffield is a man without a planet by the time he meets Lindsey on his way to Heaven's Gate Space Station. Lindsey quickly determines that the nervous guy sitting next to her is a high ranking government official on the run from one of history's most repressive governments, the totalitarian theocracy otherwise known as the North American Federation. She decides to help him and introduces Lazarus to some of Luna's finest citizens. So begins Book One of Shadow on the Moon.

ISBN 978-1-938586-06-4 Paperback

ISBN 978-1-938586-01-9 eBook

Evolution's Child - Lunarian

Book Two: Tempel Dugan leads a group of Lunarians against impossible odds. They call themselves Quan Kiai. These young warriors, and a few more like them, are all that stands between the Republic of Luna and total annihilation but things are not always as they seem.

ISBN 978-1-938586-07-1 Paperback

ISBN 978-1-938586-02-6 eBook

Evolution's Child - Thread

Book Three: The Republic of Luna is teetering at the point of collapse when the Lunarian General Council commits their last hope. They send Quan Kaia and the remaining Lunarian warriors against the Brotherhood. Fight or die. They fight in their great underground cities, they fight cross the surface of the moon, and they fight in orbital space. Earth and Luna become locked in humanities first interplanetary war, the Shadow War.

ISBN 978-1-938586-08-8 Paperback

ISBN 978-1-938586-03-3 eBook

Out of the Cradle

Where will we get our electricity when the oil and coal are gone? Why should I care? Abundant cheap electricity is a key element in getting and maintaining high human living standards around the globe. Stated another way, electricity is the foundation of modern technology. Without it, we go back to sailing ships and the horse. Out of the Cradle summarizes the major issues facing the world today and lays out a solution to our global energy needs.

ISBN: 978-0-983750-64-2 Hard Cover

ISBN: 978-0-983750-68-0 eBook

ISBN Color Version: 978-1-938586-71-2 Paperback 8.5 x 11

www.ingramcontent.com/pod-product-compliance
Lightning Source LLC
Chambersburg PA
CBHW070826180626
46818CB00001B/407

* 9 7 8 1 9 3 8 5 8 6 7 2 9 *